A
Historical
Romance Anthology

Romancing My Lady

NANCY PIRRI

ONE MAGICAL NIGHT

Marcus Calhoun returns home after divorcing his unfaithful wife. He renews his friendship with spinster, Anne Prentice. Marcus soon discovers his friendship with Anne has changed to love. Due to an imperfection, Anne can't believe Marcus loves her, until Marcus manages to prove his feelings.

ONE MAGICAL NIGHT

'Give All to Love
    Obey thy Heart'

— RALPH WALDO EMERSON

Early November 1888
A Summit Hill Mansion, St. Paul, Minnesota

A nne Preston sat quietly on a velvet divan beside her Aunt Mildred, at the Calhoun family residence. Suddenly the sound of breaking glass tore Anne out of her boredom.

"What in the world..." her aunt began, staring toward the banquet table where several servants had been working. A serving woman stood with a horrified expression on her face, mouth agape at the glasses she'd dropped from her tray.

Shards of glass glistened where they lay scattered across the ballroom floor, the servants working quickly to sweep them up. During the pandemonium, a man stood head and shoulders above the other guests. Anne's eyes widened and her heart raced when she saw the reason for the accident; it appeared the Calhoun's eldest and only son, Marcus Hall Calhoun III, had come home, after three-years' absence.

The servants finished cleaning up the mess and now stood stock-still and silent, as did the musicians and guests.

Marcus was still darkly handsome, still unorthodox in appearance with his hair falling to his shoulders. Yet, he was dressed appropriately for the occasion, his massive shoulders clad in austere black. Sparkling white accents in his shirt and cravat made a stark contrast against his attire and coloring.

Anne smiled when she saw the low-heeled shoes on his feet instead of fashionably tall-heeled boots most men of the day wore to increase their height. His head, covered in dark hair, was just a fraction below the archway. Contrarily, Marcus had tried unsuccessfully since adolescence to conceal his impressive height due to most people's reactions upon meeting him—awe, mixed with fear.

She had never feared her gentle giant. He'd always been her savior, had always protected her, until three years ago, when he married Priscilla Ames, of the prestigious banking family of New York City, and moved away. It had been considered a perfect match —the banking family marrying into the Calhoun railroad dynasty.

"Pray, do not look at him." Her aunt fluttered her fan across her bosom. "For heaven's sake, girl, at least pretend you are enjoying yourself."

Aiming a false smile toward the dance floor, Anne said, "I shall, now that Marcus has arrived." A chill swept up Anne's spine and she added, "Auntie, please, pause your fanning. I am freezing."

"Poppycock," her aunt said huffily. "Lord, but it's hot. The Calhouns should open a window or two."

Up until this moment, Anne had been tense, and miserable, her gloved hands clutched into fists. Oh, how she hated these soirees! For the third season since her coming out at eighteen years, she had been forced to sit beside her maiden aunt at social events, a false but brilliant smile pasted on her lips, waiting for gentlemen to sign her dance card.

She couldn't dance as the other girls did, for she had been born with a limp that hindered such enjoyment, though her aunt had insisted she at least try—if she were asked. But no man ever approached her. Truth be told, she'd been left on the shelf at the ripe old age of twenty. Anne was inclined to believe she would forever remain a spinster. Her aunt had other ideas, though, and had insisted she have one final season before going into "seclusion." Lord, one would think she was on death's door rather than just a wallflower.

Anne kept the smile on her face even as she rose from the divan. She took one small step but stopped when she felt a tugging on her skirts. She looked back and found Aunt Mildred's hand clutching it.

"Where do you think you're off to?" her aunt inquired.

"To find out about those windows, of course."

"Why, you can't do that. It would be impolite!" her aunt protested.

"But you said—"

"Never mind what I said and sit down."

"I'm going to greet Marcus."

Her aunt tugged fiercely at Anne's skirts, forcing her to sit.

"I won't allow you to chase after that rakehell. Our family name will be besmirched if you do."

Anne arched one eyebrow. "Why? Because he divorced

Priscilla?"

"That is only one reason."

"Or, perhaps because he made a fuss when he learned the babe Priscilla birthed was not his child?"

"Good grief, girl, stop it!"

"Or, perhaps it was the duel with Priscilla's lover," Anne said.

When her aunt's face turned a mottled red Anne decided she had better not say another word or face the consequences if she did. Her aunt had always been quick to anger and never spared the rod on her niece.

Her aunt snapped, "Heavens, he injured the man, and a duke from England no less! Marcus is very lucky the man lived."

"All you have heard are rumors, Aunt Mildred. Let us give the poor man the benefit of the doubt before we judge him." Anne rose to her feet once more. "Marcus and I have been friends since childhood. He's always treated me kindly when others have not."

Her aunt stumbled to her feet. "I won't allow you to speak to him, I said."

Anne narrowed her eyes. "Oh, but the choice is mine, not yours. Besides, I've yet to dance this evening. And I plan on enjoying myself for the remainder of it—immensely."

Anne looked away from her aunt, noting the expressions on the faces of the guests; some filled with curiosity, others with disdain, all still staring at Marcus. Silence filled the ballroom.

Though the "coming out" season had been interrupted because of the impending holiday season, Anne had still been obliged to attend this ball with her aunt. She was utterly thankful for the six-week reprieve but cringed at the thought of the season resuming after Christmas. She'd been trying to find a way to avoid similar social events but had yet to arrive at an excuse.

Beneath her sapphire taffeta skirt, her slight deformity wasn't noticeable, one limb being shorter than the other. She had felt utterly wretched and self-conscious moments ago as she watched other young ladies, accompanied by handsome young men, dancing across the shiny wood floor. Fortunately, her melancholy had fled upon seeing Marcus. Anne stood straight as she could in an effort to minimize Marcus's height advantage over her small stature. Tilting her chin, she plucked up her skirts and carefully made her way across the expanse of ballroom toward Marcus, her aunt's protestations fading as she crossed the room with small steps, trying to minimize her limp.

Her heart gladdened when his eyes lit up at the sight of her and he took two halting steps in her direction.

Marcus smiled at the sweet vision moving toward him, her sapphire gown simple and unadorned, yet tasteful. Long white gloves to her elbows lovingly encased her pretty arms. Sweeping this charming friend of his youngest sister into his arms and whisking her around the dance floor appealed to him. He loved socializing with Miss Anne Preston and had no doubt she would cheer him up. Her wry sense of humor always managed to help him see the lighter side of things.

He took in her auburn curls, the glittering blue eyes, and her perfect bow-shaped mouth. Anne had changed, he decided, sweeping an intent look over her body. The baby fat had disappeared and now a beautiful woman with pretty, gentle curves stood before him.

Anne was like a sister to him and had always been a good friend. But suddenly he wondered what it would be like to want more from her. *Impossible*, he chastised himself. He shook away his wayward thoughts and took her small, delicate hands in his large ones, careful not to crush them.

"Dance with me," she said, her sweet voice washing over him.

His smile widened. He couldn't help it, he truly couldn't. The woman had always had the ability to make the sun come out for him, even on the gloomiest of days. Laughing aloud he drew her into his arms and proceeded to dance with her, careful of her frailty. He didn't notice the lack of music at first but when he did, he scowled toward the musicians who started playing again. Soon the other guests joined in the dancing.

"You look marvelous," he murmured.

"So do you," she said bluntly, giving him a saucy smile.

As they danced, his gaze never left her face which had turned a rosy-pink color, causing her freckles to come to the surface. God, how she had hated them, while he'd always thought them adorable.

"So, sweet Anne, have you been staying out of trouble?" he inquired.

She raised her brow. "Now, who's calling the kettle black?"

His eyebrows shot up. "Tell me you don't believe all of those ridiculous stories you've heard about me."

"Tell me not a one of them isn't true."

He sighed. "I'm afraid I can't do that. I've changed, Anne. I'm not the same man you've known and idolized for years," he said dryly.

"Of course you are," she snapped. "Stop speaking nonsense."

His smile slid away. Unconsciously, he tightened his hand around her tiny waist.

Anne gasped, dropped her skirt, and placed her hand against his, fingers curved as she tried prying loose from his harsh grasp. Her lips trembled and then her body. "Stop, Marcus. You're hurting me."

He released the pressure and drew her close against him, but gently. She plucked up her skirts once more and moved carefully in his arms.

His lips brushed the top of her ear. "Sorry, sweet, I didn't mean that. It's just that—"

Anne pulled back and stared into his eyes. "What?"

"*She* always told me I was ridiculous."

"You are speaking of…"

"My wife, yes."

"Oh!" She groaned. "I'm sorry, Marcus. You do know I was only teasing you, don't you?"

"Don't worry. I'll live on without her."

The dance ended too soon for Marcus's taste, but it didn't matter. He would just dance another with her, but first he required a glass of something that would help him forget his troubles. He took her hand and walked with her across the ballroom, to the refreshment tables. "Champagne?"

Anne covertly looked around and gave a quick nod.

Marcus laughed as he handed a glass of pale gold champagne to her then plucked one up for himself. "Don't worry. Your aunt is being entertained as we speak, by my sisters."

"Thank heavens." Anne took a quick sip, then a longer one.

"Easy now," Marcus warned. "I've a feeling you aren't used to imbibing in spirits."

Anne just laughed and took another healthy sip. "I should have known Emily and Beth would have intervened."

"Really? Now why do you think they did that, do you suppose?" He looked with interest at Anne's sudden, discomfited expression.

"Bluntly put, your sisters have always wanted us to—"

"Wanted us to what?"

"Oh, don't be so wretchedly oblique! You know what." She set her glass down on a table.

"Ah, but I don't," he drawled, bending close to her ear. "But I believe I can make an accurate guess. Shall I?"

Anne grabbed his hand and pulled him along with her, drawing him out to the veranda.

"There are too many eavesdroppers, I'm afraid."

Marcus laughed aloud when she sat upon a wicker divan. He joined her, and a jolt of pleasure shot through him when his thigh touched hers. She moved away from him, to the opposite end of the divan. He wanted to pursue her, why, he had no idea. Perhaps it was because she no longer resembled a young girl.

She smoothed her skirts, then primly folded her hands in her lap. "Now you may speak."

He inclined his head, keeping his laughter at bay. She was a sly little thing and cheeky. He'd always liked that about Anne. "I was about to say my sisters are playing matchmaker, aren't they?"

Anne nodded miserably. "Yes, they have always wanted us to be together, which is an utterly ridiculous idea."

Ridiculous. There was that word again. He thought over the idea of the two of them together and didn't think it all that ridiculous.

"Why?" His eyes traveled lower as he gazed upon her slim, delicate throat and the gentle curves of her shoulders; the smooth, creamy skin of her sweetly curved breasts revealed by her décolletage.

She blustered, "Because, because, well, we grew up same as siblings, that's why!"

"Not quite," he said dryly.

He sank against the back of the divan and heard it creak. With a sigh he came to his feet, not wanting to break his mother's furnishings. He moved to the railing and stared out across his family's lawn. He knew he had been blessed to have been born into a loving family, able to provide well for him and his sisters.

The stab of guilt hit him hard then as he thought about his father's sad expression upon hearing of the duel and his failed marriage. Perhaps he should have tried harder to make his wife love him. And perhaps he should have kept hold of his temper, too, but then he couldn't decline the Duke's challenge. And, in the end, he'd only injured the man. Ironically, Marcus found himself feeling sympathetic toward the Duke of Eddington since he would now be the unlucky man to have to deal with Priscilla's nagging and temper.

"Marcus?"

He whirled around to see Anne rising. "I'm chilly. We should go back inside."

"Soon. We have a conversation to finish first."

He pulled off his coat and draped it around Anne's shoulders, smiling down at her wide-eyed expression. Then he lounged back against the railing.

Casually, he said, "Would you do me the great honor of—"

"Yes?" Anne said breathlessly, interrupting him.

"—allowing me to call on you?"

"Oh, why…why of course you may. Good heavens, Marcus, you do not even have to ask. We are friends, after all. Call away!"

He laughed but had heard the disappointment in her voice with the first sentence she had uttered. What had she expected him to say?

"Wonderful. We will renew our friendship and have great fun together."

"Fun, hmm?" she said. "Why do I get the feeling you are asking me to fill much of your time so that no other woman will tempt you?"

He stared at her until she looked away, and he wondered what Anne's true feelings were for him.

"Would that please you?" he asked.

Her winsome smile caused his heart to skip a beat.

"Yes, it would please me very much."

He cleared his throat then and said, "Come inside before you freeze to death."

She removed his jacket and handed it to him, then plucked up her skirts.

Inside, he bowed, left her, and made his way to the library, where he knew he would find his father.

Aunt Mildred grabbed Anne's hand and dragged her behind a pillar. "I can't believe you accompanied that man outside, and alone!"

"Oh, Auntie, we were just catching up on old times, that's all."

Slap!

Anne gasped, reached up and rubbed her cheek, wary but not at all surprised by her aunt's attack. She'd struck her before.

"Do not ever disobey me again, young lady. Do you understand? Never!" her aunt blustered.

Anne stood rigid, slowly lowered her hand to her side and lifted her chin. "That was unwarranted, Auntie. I shall call for our carriage."

"I am not ready to leave. You shall stay here until I am," Aunt Mildred ordered.

"Not bloody likely, ma'am," Anne snapped in a blazing tone completely uncharacteristic of her. She turned away and limped awkwardly from the ballroom. She heard her aunt shouting behind her, but she ignored her, vowing to never return to her aunt's home. She was through with the bitter old crone's abuse and would find another place to stay.

❧

Marcus stood across from his father, the large mahogany desk between them.

"Your mother is ecstatic about your return, Marcus, though I have to confess I have my reservations."

Narrowing his eyes on his father, who sat upright in his chair, hands folded in front of him on the desk, Marcus knew precisely where this conversation was headed. He did not like it.

"Say it, Father. Say it and get it off your chest."

Marcus Calhoun II rose to his feet, came around the desk and leaned against it.

The men were similar in height and breadth, but where Marcus III had been born with the same dark hair and eyes of his mother, his father possessed wavy white hair, once blond, and brilliant blue eyes. But the facial features were nearly identical.

"I think you should have stayed in New York. I believe you should have tried harder to mend your marriage."

Marcus protested, "Damn, Father, you have no idea what havoc Priscilla created in our union. Perhaps I should have stayed to continue managing the office there, but I had no choice once the Duke of Eddington called me out. And, afterward, I couldn't stay! What in the hell was I supposed to do?"

"Found another way—a gentlemanly way to solve the problem," his father snapped. Then he sighed. "What, I have no idea, yet I wonder if you truly gave the problem much thought before reacting to the situation. I have tried for years drumming into your head that acting and not reacting is the appropriate way to manage things."

"The New York office was successful," Marcus said defensively. "You can't deny it."

"Yes, with your efforts there I can find no fault, except for the fact that I now must find another competent manager to manage the office."

"Jonathon Cambridge would be perfect. He has been my second in command for three years."

"Yes, I have thought about him. But I am of the mind, upon investigating him, that he is too much like you. I can't afford to have reactionary men working for me."

"So, are you saying you have no place for me here?"

His father's gaze softened even as he took a step toward him and extended his hand. Marcus clasped it gratefully and they shook hands.

"No, not at all. Welcome to the St. Paul office, son."

❧

Anne limped through the snow, cursing inside as dampness seeped into her shoes. The dainty kid leather shoes were not meant for such wet conditions, but she was adamant about not returning to her aunt's home. No more would she take such abuse from the nasty old woman. How could this woman be her mother's sister, she mused, having often pondered this question over the past ten years, since her mother's demise.

The streets were quiet, as one would expect so late in the evening.

She couldn't trudge on any longer, she decided, especially since she had no idea of where she was headed. She had reached a park, and she sank gratefully down on the wooden bench. She shivered and scowled up at the sky. Snow was falling heavily now, blanketing the brownish icy banks and walkways from the first snow two weeks past.

As she sat, she pondered her predicament, sorrow overwhelming her. Here she was, on a wet snowy night, very near to her favorite holiday with no home to call her own.

She was still in the Calhoun's neighborhood for she had not walked but a few long blocks. But she truthfully had nowhere to go. Her few girlhood friends, including Marcus's sisters, were married with homes of their own. She knew they would welcome her, but she would never think to impose upon them.

Not for the first time did Anne think over her situation and how to make a living for herself. She'd left her aunt several months ago, checking herself into a downtown hotel. She had been gone a mere day when Aunt Mildred begged her to come back, apologizing. Never again would she return to her aunt, whether she asked prettily or begged.

Anne hadn't been allowed to finish school but had learned to be a perfect homemaker from one of her aunt's friends. She supposed she could keep house for a family or be a nanny. She smiled, thinking how much she adored children but knew her life would likely never include any.

Who would want to marry an imperfect woman like her?

She was an excellent seamstress and decided she could possibly secure a sewing position in any one of the warehouse textile factories along the river, also. But now she faced the more immediate problem of finding a place to stay.

The sound of horse's hooves caught her attention and she stared toward the street just as a fine carriage pulled by a dark horse came prancing by. It was Marcus, likely headed for the Calhoun family's townhome, near Irving Park, his place of residence when he came home to visit. Rising quickly to her feet she cupped her hands around her mouth and called out, "Marcus!"

His head snapped in her direction and he slowed down as he passed her. Anne moved toward the street, stepped down off the curb and came to a stop. She saw him turn the horse around at the corner and sweep back up the street. He stopped directly in front of her and glared down at her from his perch.

"What in bloody hell are you doing out here, Anne?" he growled. "I thought you were at my home with your aunt. And it's after midnight."

She gave him a timid smile but bristled at his words, guessing she was in for a good, long lecture.

"I required a long walk."

"Without your aunt, a chaperone, or companion?" He swept her a cursory look and added, "And you're not dressed for this abysmal weather, either. Come up and I will take you home."

Anne stepped back from the curb and jammed her hands deeper into her cloak's pockets. "I haven't a home any longer."

"What do you mean? Come, Anne."

She took another step back from his cool, irritating demand. "I will not be returning to Aunt Mildred's."

He sank back in his seat and held the reins taut in his hands. "Why not?

"I've decided I require a place of my own."

"And you will, once you marry. Did you and your aunt have an argument?"

Anne felt tears glistening in her eyes. "Yes, about you, if you must know."

Marcus sighed. "You know your aunt has never approved of me."

"True." She tilted up her chin and bravely said, "May I come home with you?"

Marcus started coughing vehemently at her question. His first instinct was to reply, *of course you may*, but then he thought about her reputation, which he had no desire to ruin.

"Just for tonight," she begged.

He jumped down from the carriage, landing directly in front of her. He smiled when she backed further away from him. Anne could use a bit of discipline, he decided, and perhaps she saw that very idea lurking within him. He'd never lay a harsh hand on her though; she was his sweet Anne and would forever hold a special place in his heart.

Taking her arm, he guided her to the carriage and assisted her up onto the seat, passing the reins to her. He took his place beside her and took back the reins. He snapped them, and they were on their way.

When he turned down the street headed for her aunt's home she protested, "I told you, Marcus, I can't return to my aunt. Please, just let me spend the night with you. Then, tomorrow, I will find another place to stay."

He pulled to the side of the street and stopped the horse, turning to her. "The truth. What happened at the ball this evening between you and your aunt?"

Anne bit her lip hard, but finally said, "She...she struck me."

Fury burst through Marcus. "She what?"

"You heard me. It is not the first time, but I've decided it most definitely is the last."

"Anne," he said softly, stroking her cheek. "I had no idea."

"It is not something I speak of publicly."

"Of course you won't go back there," he soothed.

He stared at her, but she wouldn't look him in the eyes, until he lifted her chin with a gloved hand. His heart lurched when he saw the tears pooling, angry that he hadn't realized how unhappy Anne had been living with her aunt all these years since her mother's death. Sadly, Anne had never known her father. Still, Marcus found it difficult to believe her aunt would abuse her.

Within minutes Marcus drove past his townhouse and made his way around the back. He stopped outside the stable and a young groom ran out to secure the horse and carriage.

Marcus escorted Anne inside. He helped her remove her cloak and she gave him a grateful smile. Sudden heat, especially in his nether regions, tore through his body at the sweet, thankful look on her face. Lord, but he could, he knew, take advantage of her at the moment because she was grateful to him, but he wouldn't. She was like a sister to him, for God's sake! *Of course she is. Keep telling yourself that.*

Marcus turned away, walked down a dark hall and into the parlor. There he hung her damp cloak to dry near the hearth, where a warm, welcoming fire burned. He whirled around when he heard her voice.

"Where are your servants, Marcus?"

"I don't usually have servants about in the evening hours. They have families of their own to go home to," he said.

"Oh, it is most gracious of you to allow that," she replied.

He shrugged. "They're employed by my father and will be returning to my parents' home once I hire a few servants to assist me here now that I've returned."

Marcus heard the wobbly tone in her voice and knew now she was having second thoughts about being alone with him, but she need not worry; he would never harm her or think to entice her into his bed.

Liar! Once again, the voice inside him bellowed.

"Come, warm up by the fire."

She made her way to the oversized divan, built to accommodate his size. It was positioned just across from the hearth and he smiled when she sank down with a grateful sigh. The plump divan seemed to swallow up her small form and her feet didn't touch the floor. Marcus gulped when she lifted her legs and tucked them up on the seat cushion.

He moved to the opposite end of the divan and sat down, hugging the one arm, not wanting to alarm her.

Marcus had no doubt she was an innocent, untouched woman.

She just smiled at him as she removed her damp felt hat and set it down on the floor at her side. He followed her gaze then when she turned to stare at the golden flames in the hearth, mesmerized.

He cleared his throat. "A hot toddy will help warm you. I'll prepare us one."

"That would be lovely," she murmured, still gazing into the fire.

Marcus mixed the toddies, after fetching hot water from the kitchen. He set hers down on the table near her elbow and sat down beside her again. He smiled when she leaned sideways, savoring the aroma with her small nose, then picked up her cup. Tentatively she took a sip and sighed appreciatively before taking another, then setting her cup down.

Anne was quiet, unlike his sisters and other girls he knew; she didn't spoil that worthy trait now. He found himself clearing his throat again, trying to find a way to open the doors to conversation. She couldn't stay here except for this night, but he worried about where she would live if not with her aunt. She had few friends, and the ones she had were all married. No men friends ever seemed to be about, and for the life of him, he couldn't understand why not. She was beautiful in a natural, gentle way, with nothing ostentatious about her. She possessed a wonderful sense of humor and seemed to be, for the most, good-natured. So, why in the hell hadn't some man married her yet? He found it difficult to believe a man would overlook a precious jewel due to a limp, which to his mind was a small imperfection.

"Anne? We do need to discuss what will happen tomorrow with you and your life. Have you any particular plans? Perhaps nursing school would be a good idea? I'm willing to assist you in paying for it since I've a feeling your aunt will be cutting the purse strings. What do you think?"

Nothing.

Marcus frowned when she didn't reply. Leaning forward, he

saw that she'd closed her eyes. Listening, he heard the soft cadence of her even breathing.

She'd fallen asleep. Now what was he to do with her?

He should feel insulted for never had he put a woman to sleep —to bed, but not to sleep.

He finished his drink and watched her, the small voice inside him saying he could easily carry her up the stairs and to his bed. *No! What a foolish thought.* But it was also very tempting, too.

Erotic thoughts filtered in and out of his brain, making him aware of her femininity more than ever before. He'd fought down those feelings for years, all the while wondering why she'd prized his friendship when he was nothing but a big clumsy lummox of a man. He'd sowed plenty of wild seeds in his day, though he'd always been careful not to father a child from any of those sowings.

He'd had such high hopes of having a happy marriage and raising a brood of children, but his wife's desertion and cuckolding had made him furious, then utterly miserable. The fact that, upon their wedding night, she wouldn't have a thing to do with him should have been a warning. Unfortunately, he hadn't heeded his doubts but had decided his wife had been an innocent, fragile woman-child, making love for the first time. How wrong he'd been. And in the end, he discovered she'd only married him to save her family's fortune.

Somehow, the thought of fathering a child with Anne was appealing, too much so for his peace of mind. A sick feeling came over him when he thought about how horrid and appalled, she'd be, feeling him rutting between her limbs. Anne was too pure, too good and kind for the likes of him.

But it was his duty to marry and produce an heir soon. Heaving a deep sigh, he guessed sweet Anne would never have a thing to do with him romantically. They'd been friends for too long.

He rose, raised her shoulders, and jammed a pillow beneath her head. Then he tucked a blanket over her shoulders deciding she'd be comfortable here for the night.

On his way to his bedroom he snatched up a bottle of fine Irish whisky and a glass, deciding it would be best for them if he drank himself into oblivion, otherwise he'd remain awake the entire night, tempted to seduce Anne.

⚜️

Anne groaned and punched her pillow, opened her eyes, and saw red velvet. Sitting up with a start she glared at the unfamiliar pillow then darted a quick look around the room. Breathing easier as memory returned, she was relieved she was still in Marcus's townhouse.

She smiled and fingered the soft blanket thinking how sweet that he'd covered her up against the night's chill. But then she scowled, thinking he could have installed her in a guest room, which would have been warmer and more comfortable than a divan.

Rising unsteadily to her feet she squinted toward the window, noting it was still dark. Then her gaze moved to the grandfather clock in the corner. Three o'clock? There was much more of the night yet to sleep away. Thank heavens, for she was exhausted.

Settling down on the divan once more she curled up in the blanket as thoughts of a warm blazing fire tempted her. But she was just too tired to set one. Then the tantalizing image of Marcus asleep in his warm bed with possibly a small fire still burning in his room made her promptly sit up once more.

Why should he be warm and not her?

She scrambled from the divan and made her way through the dark toward the hallway which she knew led to a set of stairs. Thankfully, he'd left a few candles burning in holders on a table, so she picked one up and made her way upstairs to find Marcus. He could easily, with little effort, set a fire for her in a guest room, she mused, even though the voice of a vixen inside her told her how he could easily set a fire inside her, as well.

Perhaps her aunt was right. Perhaps she was an evil, naughty girl who required regimented punishment. But no, there was nothing evil in wanting to feel the warmth and strength of Marcus's arms around her; to feel him take her; to feel his manhood…

Oh, my Lord, but she was evil!

Still, as she headed up the stairs, she had a purpose in mind—to find warmth and love—to sate her lonely life. For just one night, she would have this, if she could entice Marcus to want her. She'd never played the siren before but would now.

She walked down the hallway, stopping before a door where she heard the soft, deep slumbering noises of a man inside. Slowly, she turned the knob, swung open the door and closed it softly with nary a sound.

Anne paused at the foot of his bed and saw that he'd kicked off the covers. Heat seeped into her cheeks when she looked upon his naked form; he was everything beautiful, manly, and strong, the great protector she knew him to be. He'd protected her and cared for her during childhood and she knew he'd be caring and protective of her now. But once she slipped in beside him, she prayed he'd want her and not turn her away. She'd be mortified if he did!

Quickly, she removed every stitch of her clothing then slid into the bed. He didn't waken, and as she lay stiffly beside him, alcohol fumes reached her senses.

She smiled. The man had drunk himself into a stupor.

Why had he done that? To forget about her sleeping on his divan downstairs, perhaps?

Lying on her back, she reached out a searching hand, found the warm skin of his back turned toward her. Lightly, with her fingertips, she stroked him from his massive shoulders to his waist, pausing whenever he moved. She didn't want him to waken fully for he would stop her from her wanderings once he realized her identity.

She stifled a surprised shriek when he suddenly rolled over and pulled her fully into his embrace, then proceeded to nibble on her ear.

The sweet, pungent smell of alcohol made her stomach clench, yet she smiled, confirming her suspicions; he wanted her. In the past, he may have thought of her as a sister, but buried deep inside, she suspected his feelings for her were quite different.

She sighed when his big hand shoved her head beneath his chin, and she tried to make out his murmurings. Then he caught her curls between his fingers and massaged her scalp, which felt heavenly. Her heart lurched when his fingers untwined from her hair and slid down her back then up, his strong hands massaging it. She couldn't help releasing a deep groan of satisfaction. Lord, but his hands worked their magic on her tight muscles, loosening them until she felt weak and pliant in his arms.

He paused then, and his body stiffened.

No! He couldn't waken fully now.

She felt him shift and move slightly away from her. His fingers gently fingered her earlobes then drifted down her neck until he reached her breasts. She closed her eyes and gasped softly when he cupped each mound in his big hands, thumbs caressing her nipples until they peaked into hard hot pebbles. Unwillingly, she groaned once more in pure delight.

"Do you like that, sweetheart?"

Anne's eyes popped open. In the darkness she couldn't see his eyes, but he sounded awake.

"Tell me you want me," he insisted.

The heat in his voice melted away her hesitancy. "I do."

His growl of male wanting was deep and harsh, and his breathing quickened as his hands continued their exploration over her body. "It's been too long, you know. Don't deny me again, wife, not ever again."

Now Anne knew he was truly drunk for he thought she was his wife. But she wouldn't disillusion him now—she couldn't. Call her selfish, but she'd take this one moment of sweetness and hold this night's joys within her heart for years to come.

One hand left her breast, slid over her side and to her back once more, then slid down her back to end at her buttocks. He cupped and squeezed then pulled her up tight against his body.

"Do you understand?" he asked again, his voice deep, his words slurred. "Answer me."

"Yes, yes," Anne whispered. "I will never deny you."

He lit a fire deep inside her virgin body, his hands settling upon every crevice and curve, every hill and valley. Oh God, she wondered how she'd ever live without this, knowing she'd remember this night for all of her long lonely days and nights.

Soon, his breathing was as ragged as hers and he rose above her and without pause plunged deep inside her.

Anne cried out, unprepared for his sudden attack, for that's what it was; was this how much he hated his wife, that he'd attack her this way in lustful fury? The initial burning pain subsided somewhat as she lay perfectly still beneath his body covering her.

He paused, embedded to the hilt deep inside her as he calmed his ragged breathing. And then she knew he knew, in that precise moment, that she wasn't his wife. He raised his head and she felt him staring down at her in the darkness. Coming to a decision after a long while, he pulled back, then plunged forward once more but more gently this time.

"My God," he whispered wretchedly near her ear. "I can't stop now. Forgive me."

She gasped and shifted her hips, biting her lips to keep silent. Certain now that he'd breached her virginity, he moved gently inside her. This joining between them, which had initially been painful, was now exquisite. She would never regret it. She hated the idea that he would, but it was too late to stop now.

Marcus buried his head in that soft, sensitive place between her jaw and collarbone and released his passion, his body moving over her more quickly now. She felt him growing harder, larger, groaning when a sensation—a growing, welcoming heat—settled in her core. Then he lifted off her slightly, slid his big hand between their bodies and she gasped with pleasure when his fingers strummed that sensitive place between her thighs.

Her world spiraled out of control and she clasped him to her, moaning as she fell into an abyss of sexual pleasure filled with moistness, sweetness, and pure, undiluted ecstasy.

He pressed inside her one final time, finding his own joy, releasing a vivid, low growl. Then he lay upon her. Anne stroked the moistness on his back, smiling to herself. For the first time in a very long time, she felt content with her life even though her future was unknown.

Sated, they fell asleep in each other's arms.

The first words he spoke to her upon awakening were not a surprise. He lifted his head from near her shoulder and she felt his lips near her ear.

"Sweetheart?" he said, his voice hot and low, "You are not my wife because if you were, I would never have divorced you."

Gladness soared through Anne and tears filled her eyes at his words, yet she felt sorrow that he'd experienced so much sadness in his marriage. He heaved a deep sigh and rolled to his back. "Why didn't you stay on the divan, Anne?"

"I...I was cold," she said softly, scrambling to sit up. Reaching down she searched for the edge of a blanket but soon found herself flat on her back and staring up into Marcus's eyes. He'd lit a lamp on the bedside table, and she viewed his angry expression with trepidation.

"That's all you have to say?" he snapped. "Why didn't you stop me?"

Anne sniffed and stared down at her arms which she'd folded protectively against her breasts. "Because I didn't want you to."

"But you were a virgin! You should have told me."

She smothered her smile as he rose from the bed, and she watched his huge, perfectly formed body stride back and forth from the head to the foot of the bed in growing agitation. He'd always done that, she knew, that pacing when he was deep in thought. Finally, she decided she had to say something to calm him. She didn't want him feeling any regrets for she certainly didn't.

"Yes, I was. Can't you just accept my gift graciously, Marcus?"

He turned to her. "I *am* honored—and *very* grateful."

Anne saw the sincerity in his eyes and smiled. Then her gaze darted down to his groin and she was surprised to see how small he was. Moments ago, he'd been huge and had felt hard as a sword's blade.

Chagrinned, he met her eyes. "Yes, it does deflate somewhat, afterward, but just the thought of what we did together will change that shortly. Now, then, you've some explaining to do."

"From the moment you...you joined with me," she said, "you knew I wasn't your wife."

"Not at first. You are remarkably similar in size to my wife. But it's true that Priscilla wasn't virginal, even upon our wedding night. Yes, I knew then at that moment you were not Priscilla." He paced again and raked a shaky hand through his hair. "But now we've a twofold problem. You have no home, and there's a possibility you could, at this moment, be carrying my child."

"Oh!" Anne scrambled from the bed and yanked the bedsheet free, wrapping it around her body. She stood across from him on the opposite side of the bed, her eyes wide. "But that can't possibly have happened, after all, we were together just once."

"And that's all it takes, I'm afraid." He moved around the bed and stopped directly in front of her. His gentle eyes stared down at her for the longest time and Anne felt heat seeping into her cheeks again. He stroked the crown of her head then slid his hand down the smooth column of her neck and the curve of her shoulder.

"I wouldn't be averse to the idea of you blessing me with a babe."

Anne had been staring at the dark fur on his chest, wanting to reach up and stroke the hard, sinewy muscles. He was so extraordinarily handsome she had to mentally hold back from touching him. His words kicked her like a bull.

"But we aren't married!"

"We could find a judge or pastor with little problem."

Happiness filled her heart at his words, still she said, "But you just ended an awful marriage, Marcus, why in the world would you want to enter into that state again?"

He shrugged. "You are a known quality, my dear, and you are not Priscilla."

His were not the words Anne wanted to hear. She wanted what every silly woman—young or old—desires from the man she loves, for love him she did. She wanted to hear words such as "I can't live without you," or "you are the love of my life, forever and ever." But she knew she wouldn't hear them from Marcus. He'd been hurt by his wife's desertion, his feelings too raw with the pain of it. She guessed it would be a long time before he could trust his love to a woman again. Yet to her mind, without love, their marriage wouldn't succeed. Oh, she was quite certain she was in love with him and had been for years, but she didn't dare confess it. He'd feel trapped, she guessed, even if he'd gallantly suggested they marry. She knew he didn't mean it.

"True, I'm not a bit like your wife." She sighed. "I suppose it best I return to my aunt."

He frowned. "Didn't I just say we should marry?"

"Yes, you did, but I don't think one night together warrants such a drastic decision, and I don't believe, deep down inside, you believe so, either."

"But I took your innocence. How do you think that makes me feel?"

Anne gulped. "Guilty?"

"There is that, of course, but I'm making you an offer I wouldn't make lightly to any other woman, innocence taken or not," he snapped.

"Come, Marcus," she chided. "I am not the sort of woman to marry a man such as you."

He stiffened, back ramrod straight. "Grant it," he began, "I've lived the life of a rogue, but I can change. I *will* change."

Anne's eyes widened. "No! That's not what I meant."

"Then what?" he asked, relaxing a bit.

"I'm not…perfect," Anne replied, embarrassed beyond words. "I'm not beautiful with this red, curly, completely unmanageable hair, not to mention my limp. It was a wonderful, magical night, but the only night we'll ever have together."

She turned away, but he took her hand, kept her with him. Anne looked back, saw that his scowl was gone and had been replaced by a smile unlike any he'd ever bestowed on her. Gentle, kind, but with no signs of the sympathy she'd expected. He pulled her around to face him then he took her in his arms, his eyes sparkling with humor—and something else.

Her heart soared at the lustful look on his face. Lust she could well live with from her handsome, protective rogue. It would be enough for her. Marcus wasn't offering her love but pure lust, his name, and a home, but doubts filled her soul.

"You are as perfect as any woman, Anne. Believe it, believe in yourself. You are a beautiful, intelligent woman with much to offer a man. I want to be that man."

"But—"

His hand left her waist and stroked up her back. She shivered. Then he cupped the back of her head, leaned down, and brushed her lips with his. The kiss changed, grew wicked, leaving her reeling, left her wanting more when he lifted his head and blessed her with desire-filled eyes.

"I took your innocence and I'm not a cad. Plain and simple, we must marry."

"I can't marry you, Marcus." Speaking of plain and simple, duty was what he felt toward her. It was his duty to marry her since he'd taken the gift a bride gives to her husband. To her mind this was not enough reason to marry.

She stepped out of his arms and moved to the window, staring outside through the tears.

His low voice came to her then, cool and low. "Did you expect me to say that I'm in love with you, Anne?"

❦

Anne turned to him, abject horror creasing her sweet face. His blunt words had surprised her and now he was faced with the prospect of responding to his own question. Was he in love with her? Of course, what young woman wouldn't want and rightfully expect the man who'd asked for her hand to love her?

Marcus was honest with himself; he'd always cherished their

friendship but hadn't felt anything but familial caring toward Anne. But now he had to wonder about his judgment regarding women, especially after what great suffering he'd endured with Priscilla, whom he believed he'd loved. He'd believed she'd loved him. He knew how his father felt about his mother, how his father would risk his own life if it meant saving her. That, Marcus told himself, was true love.

"I've come to realize that I truly don't know how it feels to be in love with someone. Can you understand that, Anne?"

A tear slid down her cheek when she closed her eyes. He groaned, moved to her side, and gently stroked the cheek, following the travels of that one tear.

She opened her eyes at the touch of his hand and stepped away from him, turning her back to him once more.

Marcus stood there helplessly trying to decide what to do or what to say when she chose that moment to speak, and quite sensibly, too. So typical of Anne, though he knew how great her effort was when she was hurting inside. But he would never lie to her.

"I didn't expect you to make that sort of declaration to me, Marcus, truly I didn't. But I can't accept your proposal because you feel duty-bound to offer for me. Our marriage would be nothing but one of convenience."

He moved up behind her, yanked the sheet from her body, and pulled her back against him. She struggled in his arms, brushed his groin.

He warned, "Stop it now, unless you plan on me taking you to bed again." She stopped struggling and he held her close, his arms around her waist. Leaning down he nibbled on her earlobe until she went limp in his arms. "Feel me, sweetheart," he murmured. He slid one hand over her taut stomach, cupped one breast. "Wouldn't you enjoy spending night after night making love, our passions igniting each other? You can't deny you want me." He slid his hand down her front to end at that place between her legs. "Can you leave all of this then, especially now that you've tasted passion?" he finished.

Her breathing grew ragged and then she wrenched her body from his arms. She turned and threw herself against him, winding her arms and legs around him. He kissed her ruthlessly as he carried her to his bed. Marcus's last thought before entering her heated warmth again was that Anne would be far more than a convenience for him. And he meant to prove to her exactly that, for the rest of the evening—and afterward—for as long as it took to convince her.

Unfortunately, by the time he wakened late the following morning, she had gone. As he sat morosely at his dining room table, drinking coffee, he decided to pay her a visit that afternoon, knowing she'd returned to her aunt.

He arrived on Aunt Mildred's doorstep. Her ancient butler answered the door and escorted him, wordlessly, into the parlor. As Marcus sat there waiting for Aunt Mildred's appearance, he had a premonition that Anne was not in residence.

Mildred confirmed this upon entering the parlor. "Well, what have you done with the worthless girl?"

Without a word to the ornery woman he strode from her house then proceeded to pay calls on his two sisters, all the while praying she was with one of them. And even though both he, and Emily and Beth's husbands, threatened dire consequences if they were concealing information, neither woman confessed to knowing Anne's whereabouts.

Marcus spent the next two weeks worrying and querying everyone he knew about Anne, even going so far as to hire an investigator to find her but had no luck. As time passed, he grew deathly worried that something awful had happened to her. During her month's absence he'd contemplated his feelings about Anne, vowing to prove his love for her when he found her, for he'd learned that he truly did indeed love her.

The day before Christmas his sister Emily summoned him. Upon entering her home, he was shocked to find a very red-faced Emily standing at one end of the dining room table, eating her supper. Her husband, Brent Hawthorne, sat at the opposite end. He rose upon Marcus's entrance, moved to his side, and took his arm.

At the library door, Hawthorne paused and looked back across the hall at his wife. "Don't even think about leaving before I'm finished discussing things with your brother, Emily. Do you understand?"

Emily's face turned redder, if possible, tear-filled eyes on him and sniffed. "I won't leave." He closed the door with a decided click.

Marcus was astonished. Never had he seen his strong-willed sister quite so docile. He also wondered why she was standing and eating her supper but would never ask.

What was between husband and wife stayed there, in his opinion.

Brent sat behind his desk and waved Marcus into a leather chair. The man was one of the finest, wealthiest solicitors in St. Paul, and his home and business confirmed it. Brent and Emily had only been married a year and both of them had seemed to be truly in love. This was the first time Marcus had noted any adversity between them.

Pouring them each a snifter of Irish whisky, his brother-in-law said, "I've learned of Anne's whereabouts today. Care to hear where she's been staying?"

Marcus had been in the middle of taking a drink when he started coughing then slammed down his glass. "Of course!"

"She's at your hunting lodge up north."

"How in the world did she know where to find the place? And it's nothing but a hovel, for God's sake," Marcus growled.

"Emily instructed one of our stable boys to drive her there. I told your sister she was damned lucky she got off as easy as she did. This time of year, Anne could have been caught in a snowstorm during her travels."

"True, as a matter of fact, I can smell snow in the air now. What do you mean, got off easy?" Marcus asked curiously.

Dryly, Brent said, "There's a reason Emily is standing eating her supper. I had a feeling she knew much more than she'd admitted to us. So, when railing, wheedling, and begging didn't work, I took her over my knee."

"You... Why, now that I think of it," Marcus said, "Love taps from my father always seemed to improve Emily's behavior. He raised his brow. "But how did you know that Emily knew?"

"There was nowhere Anne could have gone—without someone's assistance. The woman has few friends, but the ones she does, like Emily, are loyal. I'd already questioned everyone who knew Anne and could tell by their responses they were truthful and had no idea of her whereabouts. Emily had a tendency to change the topic of conversation whenever I started questioning her, in effect, telling me she knew."

"You are one damned smart man, Brent," Marcus drawled as he came to his feet. "I'll go fetch Anne home."

Brent rose from behind his desk. "But you won't make it back for the holiday celebration tomorrow."

Marcus grinned. "You're right. But I've my own plans for the holiday, which should be highly interesting and entertaining. Make my excuses to the family, won't you?"

Brent grinned in return then left the library with Marcus. As the men passed through the hallway, they both paused to see Emily still standing at the table.

Grinning widely, Marcus said, "Happy Christmas, sweet sister."

Emily snapped, "Just let Anne know I did not divulge her whereabouts willingly, Marcus."

He laughed and saluted. "I will."

Christmas Eve 1889

Anne laid down her knitting, stood and peered anxiously out at the heavy falling snow. Here it was, Christmas Eve, and she sat alone and cold. She had told Emily she would stay at Marcus's hunting lodge just a month or so, until she determined whether she carried his child. Sighing, she sank down into her chair again as disappointment set in.

She'd learned yesterday she hadn't conceived. Oh, how she'd wanted that little joy in her life, though she knew she'd never be able to live with herself since Marcus would have felt obligated to marry her. As a matter of fact, she knew him well enough he'd force her into marriage, not physically but with gentle loving words of which she knew he was capable, and which she couldn't ignore.

Now she needn't worry. And she'd come to a decision over the past month. She loved him, it was a fact, and she promised herself she'd make him learn to love her and eventually want marriage as much as she did.

She'd already packed her few belongings, expecting to see Emily's stable boy arrive early tomorrow. Due to the timely nature of her woman's cycle she'd known her flow would have started by this day. She leaned forward, her arms around her middle as a cramp settled deep inside her. Oh Lord, but she hated being a woman at times like these! She'd been putting off going to bed, dreading the painful hours ahead. By tomorrow, though, she would be feeling better, she knew.

Then she heard a rumbling sound outside the cabin. She rose to her feet, pulling her woolen shawl close. Then she swiped at the fogged window, gasping to find a huge carriage and two horses standing outside. The boy was a night early. Fine, since this place had long ago lost interest for her. Besides, she didn't want to stay in this cold, lonely place any longer but craved the warmth of a house with decent furniture and a blazing fire. She'd only managed a small fire since her arrival here and her fingertips seemed always to be near-frozen.

Anne saw a man alight from the carriage and stride toward the cabin, his long black cape flying in the wind behind like a flag on a sailing ship. No! It couldn't be him!

She stood back, clutching her shawl when Marcus threw open the door, ducked beneath the doorjamb, and stood in the doorway, looking huge, healthy, and handsome—and furious.

"Marcus!" She took a step toward him.

He held up one hand, as though warding her off. "Hold up, woman, I'm nearly frozen to death and don't want you catching your death before I've warmed up." He closed the door and rubbed his gloved hands together briskly.

Anne grinned and moved to his side. "And I have no desire for you to freeze to death but to help warm you up." She threw her arms around his neck and held on tight. Satisfaction soared through her body when he wound his arms around her and held her against him. She shivered at the cold from his body but wouldn't let go. She was overjoyed to see him.

He raised her higher then and kissed her with cold lips that soon turned hot. Anne found herself grinning against his mouth. When he ended the kiss, she looked into Marcus's furious expression as he held her against his woolen coat.

Smack! A sharp pain exploded in her buttocks and she squirmed for release, but he held her even tighter. She gasped, unable to believe that Marcus would lay a hand against her. She looked at him warily.

"Yes," he murmured as he lowered her until her feet touched the floor, "you should be worried, for you've worried me for nearly three weeks. Do you know what I'd like to do with you?"

His calm tone surprised her, considering how her bottom stung from that one smack. She nodded and bit her lip, held onto his forearms as she stared up at him with wide eyes.

"Kiss you, paddle your rump, and make love to you until you never want to leave my bed."

She tossed back her head and laughed. "Oh, thank heavens you knew precisely the words I wanted to hear."

He released her, pulled off his wet coat and hat. Then, slowly, he removed his gloves, his eyes never leaving hers.

"Did I, you little minx?"

She gave him a coquettish smile and nodded.

"Of which shall I oblige you first? The kiss, the beating, or the bedding?"

Anne remembered her woman's time and sighed. "I am sorry, Marcus, for leading you on such a chase, especially in such awful weather. But I needed to think—alone."

"About…?

"Us. About your proposal."

"And?"

"I think you're absolutely right that we should marry." Anne saw a glimmer of hope in his eyes and sighed. "No, I'm not expecting a baby, Marcus."

His gentle smile widened. "We've the rest of our lives to have babies. Now then, did I hear you say you accept my proposal?"

"You did."

"And why is that, especially now since you're not carrying my child?"

"Because I love you," she said simply.

"What!" he shouted.

She nearly laughed at the belligerent look on his face. And now he stood before her, long legs spread wide, fists on his hips.

"You heard me the first time, I'm certain."

"I want to hear you say it again," he ordered.

Anne sighed. "I'm so pathetic, but I do love you, and I know it's all for naught. Do not feel obligated to give me words that will make me feel better. Do not feel guilty that you do not love me in return."

He took a step closer and Anne gasped at the raw pain in his eyes. Her hand came up and she covered her mouth, stilling her trembling lips, waiting for him to tell her again, once more, that he would never love.

"Don't say you don't—" She halted, put a hand up, warding him away but he came closer. And closer. Until he stood directly in front of her again and stared deep into her eyes.

Without a word he swept her up in his arms and carried her to the small bed in the corner. There he laid her down and sat beside her. He cupped his hands around her breasts and held them, stroking the nipples through her gown. Anne closed her eyes, enjoying his touch. But when he moved to unbutton her gown, she held his hands.

Embarrassed beyond words since she'd never had to confess such a thing to a man before, she whispered, "I can't make love to you now, Marcus."

He looked at her in confusion.

"Oh, I want to," she said hurriedly, "but I have my…" Anne covered her hot cheeks and couldn't meet his eyes.

She heard him chuckle softly as he rose to his feet.

Anne scowled. "There is nothing humorous about my...my discomfort."

"Then I shall comfort you this night and every night. Now then, sweet, let me finish what I started to say earlier. "I have always loved you. From the very beginning, from the first moment we met," he said softly.

Tears filled Anne's eyes. "How is this possible? And why did you deny your feelings to me earlier?"

"Because I am a great fool. It took you leaving and me worrying about you for the past weeks to see deep inside my own soul. I cannot live without you, Anne." He pulled his pocket watch out, checked the time. "It's midnight." He met her eyes and held out his hand to her. "Merry Christmas, darling."

Placing her hand in his, Anne would always remember this holiday, more than any other she guessed. Marcus would always be her lover, husband, friend, and protector.

He pulled her from the bed, took a seat himself, and sat her down upon his knee.

"Now then," he purred as he nibbled on one of her earlobes. "I believe it's time we welcomed in the holiday, don't you? Where were we?"

"Now, Marcus, remember my discomfort?" she said, wondering and thinking about that hard smack he'd delivered earlier.

"Ah, well, there'll be no spanking, and no making love this evening then, I'm afraid. But there's nothing to prevent me from kissing you, is there?"

She gave him a saucy grin. "Not a thing, darling."

"Precisely what I thought. Besides, it's better we leave the best 'til last."

THE END

COURTING THE NANNY

Helen Jameson turned away from the man she loved when rumors spread that he had betrayed her with another woman. Years have passed, and Helen finds herself having to serve the man she once and still loves as nanny to his twin boys, as a way to pay off her brother's gambling debts to him. Elliott Falconer has wanted to marry Helen for as long as he can remember. He forgave her for not trusting him and believing a lie. Now that he has her in his home, he hopes to rekindle the romance and make his long-time dream come true.

Author Note:
This story is also included in
Kiss Or Kill Under the Northern Lights, Vol. 1

COURTING THE NANNY

St. Louis, Missouri
September 1877

"I'm sorry to have to ask you again, sis, but as I said in my letter, I need money."

"Good heavens, Georgie," Helen Jameson replied, glaring at her brother. "What have you done?"

"Helen? Call me George. I'm too old for Georgie."

She smoothed her russet-colored skirts as she sat in the parlor of their family home. "Until you show me some measure of maturity, you will remain *Georgie*. Tell me what happened."

He paced the floor, tugging at his shirt collar nervously the whole time. "I'm not quite sure where to begin."

"From the beginning is usually a good place."

He grimaced. "I drank too much and lost everything playing cards."

"What do you mean by *everything*? Be specific, and to whom?"

"Oh, damn, you're not going to be happy to hear this."

She sighed. "I suppose I won't, but you did write to me and ask me to travel over a thousand miles to help you."

"I've lost what little I had left of my inheritance to Elliott Falconer. Even if I hadn't, it wasn't enough to cover the debt. Which is why I'm asking you for help."

Helen placed her fingers against the racing pulse in her neck. "*My* Elliott?"

He nodded. "Well, your once-upon-a-time Elliott."

Heat seeped into the core of her as she thought about her ex-fiancé; thought about his tall, dark good looks, his charm. Oh, yes, Elliott could charm a woman. But he was also one of the worst pranksters she'd ever met. Helen thought of the tricks he and her brother played on her over the years. As a boy, Elliott could brew up a barrel of trouble and her brother happily followed in the older boy's footsteps. To have to face him again would be difficult, but she had no choice.

She'd come to help George, even giving up her teaching position at Aimes Academy for Young Ladies in Upstate New York, intent upon finding suitable employment near her brother. Nothing had changed; she'd always made sacrifices for him. He was her baby brother whom she adored, yet she knew it was long past time he grew up. At twenty-four, he should be mature. Heavens, he should be *married* by now with children in his nursery. *Now who's calling the kettle black? I should be married as well.*

"Well, there's nothing we can do but pay him a visit and see if we can arrange some sort of repayment schedule," she said sensibly.

George pulled out his pocket watch and frowned. "Let me see if I can catch up with him tonight." As he headed for the door, he said over his shoulder, "Thank you, sis. I'll be forever in your debt."

Didn't she know it!

After he left, she rose from the divan and moved to one of the many windows in the parlor. Staring blindly into the night, memories flooded her, particularly those of her and Elliott's courtship and subsequent engagement eight years ago. They'd been so in love…until she'd heard accusations that Elliott had impregnated a past sweetheart, Virginia Pettigrew—one of St. Louis's wealthiest heiresses. Helen found herself convinced the gossip-mongers were to be believed instead of Elliott, and she broke off their engagement. Only later had she discovered the mistake she'd made in not believing him.

She'd fled St. Louis and moved to New York. There she'd used her inheritance to put herself through school at Wells Women's College, earning a teaching degree. After graduation, she'd secured a teaching position in Upstate New York. Much of her remaining inheritance she'd contributed to George's education to become a lawyer. She managed to live modestly on her teacher's pay and had little in savings.

Elliott had appeared at her school several times in the first few months after she'd left home, begging her to reconsider and marry him, explaining how it had all been a terrible mistake. Each time she'd informed him she never wanted to see him again.

Several months later, George contacted her and told her how Elliott had been wrongly accused. The true father had stepped forward to claim Virginia's child as his own. Elliott had been socially and legally exonerated. After that, he'd appeared on her doorstep each summer, during his travels to New York on business, but she'd been too humiliated to receive him. It was all her own doing, she knew. If she couldn't believe in him before they married, how could she afterward?

At twenty-eight, she was a spinster-schoolteacher, living a lonely existence. After Elliott, she hadn't sought to be courted, though she'd had invitations. She was convinced she'd never find a love like theirs again.

She chewed on her lower lip as she swept away from the window and paced back and forth across the red- and gold-patterned carpeting, growing more agitated by the minute when she thought about her brother's irresponsible behavior. She'd helped him out far too many times. This would be the last.

The following evening, Helen stood stock-still on one of the wharfs along the Mississippi River, staring at the magnificent steamboats. She shook her head in dismay. It was a cool autumn evening yet the cold seeping into her spine wasn't from the weather.

George reached for her hand, but she stepped back and folded her arms across her chest.

"Elliott's waiting. As it is, he had to make time this evening for us."

Her voice trembled. "Why are we meeting him on a boat?"

"He owns *The Lucky Lady*. Isn't she a beauty?"

She had to admit the boat shimmered and glittered in its white and gold magnificence due to the multitude of lights on its surfaces. She also heard lively piano music and raucous laughter. There appeared to be three levels on the boat, all filled with people dressed quite finely and partaking of food and wine.

"I assume *The Lucky Lady* is the place where Elliott offers temptations to stupid young men such as you?"

He grimaced. "I know I had that coming, but yes, this is the place."

"Well, I suppose if we must go aboard, we must."

She picked up her skirts, started across the narrow planking, and followed George. She slowed her steps and stared in horror at the water between the shoreline and boat. Finally, she stopped completely. Horrible memories enveloped her as she imagined licking flames aboard another steamboat, following a massive explosion. She shuddered.

George stared at her over his shoulder. "What is it?"

"I can't go aboard, George. Please, you go on and I'll wait in the carriage." She started backing away.

Impatient now, George said, "But Elliott's set supper for us. There's nothing to worry about. I've a feeling the outcome of this meeting will be a good one. You know how sensible Elliott has always been."

"I just can't!" She turned and fled.

※

Elliott sat on a chair before a resplendently set table in his cabin's berth, a copy of Emerson's *Society and Solitude* in his hands. A cool autumn breeze wafted through the open window. The only thing spoiling the setting was the pervasive, persistent stench of rotting fish.

The gentle swaying motion of *The Lucky Lady* relaxed him. He'd dressed formally to meet George and Helen and had set the table for supper. Succulent roasted chicken, rice, carrots, and crusty bread sat on a sideboard against one wall. He'd selected several bottles of fine wine but now had second thoughts. Helen had rarely imbibed in liquor. George had a tendency to overdo it. Quickly, he moved to the sideboard and tucked all but one bottle of wine out of sight.

He could have entertained them in one of the many salons on his boat, but it would have been difficult escaping the noise from the music and the guests. His cabin was large enough to set a table for three and yet small enough to exude intimacy. He wanted to make a good impression on the woman he'd loved for years—the woman he'd never stopped loving. The woman who refused to meet with him—until now.

Elliott heard his first mate Rory's particular knock and rose. Yanking down his gray waistcoat and brushing the shoulders of his charcoal-colored frock coat, he called out, "Enter!"

George Jameson peered inside. "You alone?" he asked, casting a covert glance around his quarters.

Elliott's grin widened. "At the moment. You're late." He leaned sideways and tried to look around George, his grin diminishing. "Where's your sister?"

"She's in the carriage, and none too happy with me at the moment."

"Or me, I would imagine," Elliott replied, thinking of Helen's magnificent temper. She'd always been slow to anger, but when she did a man would do well to stay out of her way.

"So, is she coming in?"

"I'm afraid she can't," George said.

"Why not?" Elliott tried concealing the growing impatience in his voice. He was anxious to see the woman he hadn't seen in years, not for lack of trying, though. Once a year, each time he traveled to New York for business, he made it a point to seek her out. She was never home for him.

"We should have chosen a different place to meet," George said.

"I see. I guess I can't blame her for not wanting to come aboard since this is the place where you lost all your money."

"That's not the reason. Our parents died aboard a boat similar to this one. Insensitive idiot that I am, I hadn't realized being on a boat would bother her so."

Elliott groaned. "Damn. I hadn't thought about it either, but it makes sense. Of course, I knew about the fire and their deaths, but it never occurred to me how difficult it would be for Helen to come aboard. Let's eat and discuss the debt on land."

"Yes, that would be best," George said.

Elliott left the cabin and moved down the stairs to the main deck, greeting guests along the way. He stopped beside his first mate with George behind him. "I'll be gone a few hours, Rory."

"No problem, boss."

Upon reaching the carriage, George and Elliott stood side by side and stared in at Helen through the window thrown wide open. Her eyes were closed. Elliott groaned when the light from a streetlamp caught the shimmering tears on her cheeks, and he yanked open the door.

Helen blinked and straightened on her seat. Their eyes locked. Elliott felt as though he'd gone back in time. She hadn't changed a bit. She was still tiny, still red-haired and green-eyed, still heartbreakingly beautiful. And, upon seeing her again, he realized he forgave her for breaking off their engagement. He'd been so bitter for so long, but his feelings hadn't prevented him from trying to see her every year. Perhaps the passing of time did heal things.

"Elliott," she whispered.

His heart clamored inside his chest as he felt the pull between them all over again. It had always been that way. To this day, Elliott couldn't fathom how she'd possessed the strength to break away from their love.

"Helen," he murmured. Reaching inside, he took her small gloved hand in his and eased her from the carriage until she stood directly in front of him. He was gladdened to see that her pretty eyes were wide and filled with joy and—was it possible?—longing. He felt the same way but didn't dare show her for fear he'd frighten her away.

He was unable to tell the color of her gown due to the dark but had no problem seeing how the fit of the gown enhanced her womanly shape. She wore a veiled hat atop her upswept hair. His hand itched to pull the silly thing off. He'd pull every pin from every curl once he got rid of the ridiculous hat. He remembered how, when they'd picnic together with George as chaperone, he'd tease her by pulling out the pins, ignoring her protests. Then he'd sink back on the blanket and watch her red hair cascade down around her shoulders. He gulped down the lump in his throat, recalling how she'd give him a mock scowl and scold him as she pinned her tresses up again.

He shook himself to escape the memories, tucked her arm through his, and started walking down the wharf. "Allow me to apologize for my insensitivity. Mandy's Café is right across the street. That all right, George?"

George was ambling along behind them. "Anywhere is fine with me. I'm starving."

"It'll be more comfortable than my boat."

She gave him a small, dimpled smile. "Thank you."

His nether regions started aching. It was the same reaction he'd always felt around her. As they strolled down the street, Elliott kept her close beside him. They reached Mandy's which served a small selection of exquisite entrées, and they were seated in a private corner. The serving girl recognized Elliott. The proprietor also stopped by to greet them.

In between bites of food, Helen and Elliott talked while George ate heartily and listened. After they finished eating, George looked at Helen. "We may as well get the worst part of the evening taken care of."

"I suppose," Helen said.

Elliott sank back in his chair and smiled. "There's no rush to pay off the debt. Affordable, monthly payments will be fine."

"Wonderful!" George said. "That's mighty generous of you."

"Generous?" Helen said, her voice, in Elliott's opinion, stating otherwise.

He sat forward and planted his elbows on the table. "We can come up with another more agreeable arrangement if you like."

He'd thought he was being exceedingly magnanimous until he caught the warning glint of steel in Helen's eyes.

"Excuse me, Mr. Falconer. If not for you and that floating den of iniquity, George wouldn't have gambled away all of his money."

George groaned. "It's not Elliott's fault. It's my own."

Elliott laughed.

Helen glared at him.

"Pardon me," Elliott drawled, "but I love it. It seems nothing has changed over the years. The two of us vexing your sister and driving her into a magnificent fury."

Helen scraped her chair across the wooden floor and rose. Both Elliott and George scrambled up, watching and waiting to see what she'd do next. Her scowl softened and her lips started curving into a smile.

Elliott thought, *Oh, to hear the sound of her sweet laughter again.* Then she obliged him. Her laughter was contagious, and Elliott and George followed suit as they all sank down into their chairs.

"I should have taken a stick to the two of you when you were younger," she grumbled, rearranging her skirts.

"I don't know if that would have helped us any," Elliott replied. He looked up and waved his hand. "More wine and another brandy here, Sally Mae!"

The server soon returned to the table with their beverages. After a while, George came to his feet. He gave Elliott a sheepish look and jammed his hands into his pockets. "Uh, you know I'd pay my share, but I'm broke."

"This was my idea to come here. I've got it."

Helen arched an eyebrow and stared at George. "Where are you going?"

"I've a previous engagement. There's no need to worry; I've learned my lesson well and won't be gambling again. I promise." He turned to Elliott. "Will you see Helen home?"

"Of course. I'd planned on it."

"Good night then," George said.

Elliott sank back in his chair, swirling his glass of brandy. "I'd like to ask you something, Helen."

"All right," she said hesitantly.

"Have you missed home?"

"Initially, I was dreadfully lonely. But I wanted to be a teacher and Wells was an excellent college. After I'd lived there two years, it had become home to me. After graduating, I stayed and found a teaching position at Aimes Academy. And you?" she said. "What have you been doing with your life? George has told me little."

"After you left, I...I left as well, for a while."

He'd stayed in St. Louis but had drowned himself in drinking, gambling, and in whatever fair delights women offered him.

"Then my father died, and I took over *The Sentinel News*, got married, had children." He shrugged. "Guess you could say I've lived a very normal existence."

He saw all color drain from Helen's face, and he frowned. "Helen? What's wrong?"

"You...you're married?"

"Up until three years ago."

Helen recalled George's words—how Elliott hadn't married Virginia Pettigrew, how her accusations had all been lies. So, who had he married?

"Tell me about your wife," she said in a decidedly choked voice.

"Emily died while birthing our daughter. The babe died as well."

Her heart broke at his words, but she listened intently as he told her about his satisfying years with his sweet Emily. She heard the joy in his voice when he spoke of her and their life together, and then the sadness when he told of her death. Jealousy tore through Helen when she thought about him being happily married, making love with his wife, having babies together. Then she chastised herself. He'd had every right to be happy, even if she hadn't been. But then, she'd been the one to break off their engagement even though Elliott had meant everything to her. Oh, why hadn't she listened to her inner soul about him? Why hadn't she trusted him?

Elliott reached out and took one of her hands in his. "I suppose you wouldn't have known since George was away at school and not living here at the time."

"True." She bit her lower lip a moment before adding, "I owe you an apology for not believing you all those years ago about Virginia."

He released her and sank back in his seat.

She grew uncomfortable under his long, intent stare and had no idea how to proceed.

Elliott raised a challenging eyebrow. "Yes, I believe you do need to set things right. Truthfully, you have no idea how many times I planned on taking you over my knee if I ever met up with you. Lucky for you we never did. It hurt, Helen, really hurt that you believed I'd stray from you." He raked his fingers through his hair and scowled at her. "To this day, I still wonder why you'd believe town gossip over my word. We were engaged, for God's sake, and had courted for over two years. Why would I have even thought to take up with another woman?"

Helen cringed at his sharp words, knowing he was righteous in his anger. What man didn't consider having his honor questioned the worst thing that could happen to him? She couldn't think of any reply but sat stiffly, allowing him to vent his feelings. She saw his expression change from anger to calculating—yes, she'd seen that look before, and she braced herself for his next barrage of words.

"So, I've the perfect solution, by way of an apology, and a means for you to assist George in paying off his debt to me." He looked at her, gaze steady. "I need a nanny. It would go a long way toward an apology for not believing me in the past if you cared for my children until I can find a dependable, sensible nanny."

"You…but you said your daughter died along with your wife."

"Ah, but not before blessing me with twin boys first who just turned five a week ago."

Boys? Other than her younger brother, boys were foreign to her. She taught young women at the college, so girls she understood. Still, the chance to be close to Elliott overrode all common sense and any arguments she might think of. But then she was asking for punishment and sadness if she worked for him, knowing how his feelings for her had forever changed. After all, his love for her had long ago been replaced by love for his wife.

"Helen?"

She looked up, meeting his eyes.

"What do you think? I figure in three months you'll have paid off the debt. And it would give me great relief and comfort to know my sons are in capable hands until I can find a suitable replacement."

Helen decided her life would be pure torture working for Elliott, being so close to him and knowing they couldn't be together. Still, she had no recourse but to accept. There was the debt to be repaid. But what about the possibility of her falling in love with him again? Impossible. Too much time had passed. She'd been stupid and full of righteousness, allowing time to slip away instead of apologizing. Her pride had gotten in the way of being sensible.

"All right," she said. "Shall we talk business then?"

He laid out his plan concerning her duties, the pay, hours of work per day for three months' duration. She thought everything was fair until he came to the last item—he expected her to reside in his household.

She stopped him as humiliation swept through her and she sputtered, "My living in your household you consider business? How dare you!"

Consumed by anger, it took her a moment to realize all talking and activity in the café had ceased. Now, as she gave a furtive look around, she saw the shocked and curious expressions of the other diners, her cheeks blazed in humiliation.

A chair scraped the wooden floor. She looked up and met Elliott's scowl when he threw down his napkin.

"So, I suppose this means we have no deal?" he inquired coolly.

"Have you no respect for me, Elliott?" she said, rising to her feet, facing him across the table.

He groaned. "Of course I do. You *know* I do. But *all* of the nannies I've hired have lived in my home. They're required to care for my sons twenty-four hours a day when I'm not home due to how often I travel. My cook and housekeeper leave for their own homes at the end of each day but not the nanny. I'm sorry if I offended you. You must know that was never my intention."

Somewhat mollified by his explanation, she sank into her chair once more. He took his seat as well. Guilt once again plagued her when she saw his sad expression.

"I could never live in your house. It would ruin me," she softly replied.

His suggestion had surprised her, caught her off guard. She knew Elliott, knew well how he'd always treated her with the utmost respect. But it wouldn't be proper for her to live with him, especially now that she knew his other employees left at the end of each day. All the while, though, she couldn't help but think how right it would feel to live in his household. But then only as his wife—not the nanny.

Five-year-old boys and possibly a succession of nannies caused suspicion to set in. "I get the distinct impression you've lost several nannies."

He nodded. "It's true, yes."

Helen watched him with a narrow-eyed look. He wouldn't meet her gaze but stared down at his wineglass.

She raised one eyebrow. "Now, why do you suppose that is?"

He looked uncomfortable. "They had their reasons. Personal in nature, guess you'd say."

"I see." What more could *she* say? She had her misgivings, just because of the things left unsaid by Elliott. Still, she needed the job to help George pay off the gambling debt. And there was the fact she would have an excellent excuse to be close to Elliott again. "Well, here's what I can do. I'll drive my own carriage to your house each day. I'll stay with the boys from seven in the morning until eight each evening, then return home for the night."

"That should work, but I've a favor," he said. "Will you agree to stay overnight with the boys if I need you to? Your reputation won't be ruined or even slightly tarnished since everyone knows how often I leave town on business."

She worried her lower lip, then said, "Yes, I think that will work."

He gave her the lopsided smile she'd always loved. "So, dare I say we've reached a bargain?"

She smiled in return. "I believe we have."

He gave her a relieved sigh, then picked up her hand. Warmth soared through her body when he raised it to his lips and kissed it, his eyes on hers the entire time.

"How soon can you start working for me?"

"Whenever you need me, I'm available."

Elliott groaned. "I like the sound of that."

She swatted his hand and stood up from her seat.

He laughed and rose, his expression turning serious. "I have newspaper business and need to leave for Minneapolis tomorrow morning. Can you stay with the boys for the next few weeks?"

Stunned, she stumbled out, "But...but...I...won't the boys feel uncomfortable with me, a stranger staying with them?"

"Not a bit," he assured her.

She nearly declined until she noticed the look on his face. He looked at her as if she was his savior. If there was one thing Helen couldn't resist in life, it was someone needing her.

"I'd hoped you would be here until the boys got used to me, but if it can't be helped, so be it. Yes, I'll stay at your home while you're gone."

He snatched her up in his arms and whirled her around. Helen smiled at his exuberance. He reacted as if his biggest problems had been lifted from his shoulders. When he set her down, he gave her a big smacking kiss on one cheek. The few diners burst into applause. Helen's cheeks heated up in embarrassment.

She reached for her cloak, but he got it first.

In mock sternness, she said, "Why in the world do I put up with you?"

Grinning, he said, "Because you love me, that's why."

Heat swept through her at his true comment as he draped her woolen cape around her shoulders and escorted her outside. Once he had her settled in the carriage, he climbed in after her. She held her skirts close to her legs and shifted to the opposite side, allowing him space.

His next words startled her. "You know we were always meant to be together, don't you?"

His comment was bold—meant to fluster her. She managed to calmly reply, "We were young, foolish, and so in love." She sighed. "But we had a lovely time while it lasted, didn't we?"

He scowled. "To my mind, nothing is final between us. If I'd fought harder for you, we'd likely be married now with several children. I'm sorry I wasn't more tenacious."

"You came several times after I'd left! To me, that qualifies as sincerity and tenacity on your part."

"True, but I should have been even more persistent. I shouldn't have given up."

She smiled. "I was very hurt and angry and would never have allowed you in. I regretted my stubbornness later, once I'd learned the truth from George, but by then it was too late." She gave him a curious look. "By the way, how would you have gained entrance?"

"I should have planted myself on your doorstep until you had no choice but to talk to me. I wouldn't have left simply because you wanted me to—because you told me to."

Helen's smile slipped as she listened to his words, thinking these were words of a strong man who knew his own mind, not the words of the young unsure man she'd left behind.

"Yes," he said slowly. "That's exactly what I *should* have done."

◈

The very next morning Helen arrived on Elliott's doorstep in a hired carriage loaded with two large valises.

His home was located just on the outskirts of St. Louis. It was large —meant for a large family, she decided as she waited in the parlor as the driver unloaded her trunks. Upon Elliott's instruction, he carried them up the stairs and installed them in a guest bedroom. Returning downstairs, he carried Elliott's two bags and stowed them in the coach.

Elliott paid the driver to wait for him, then went back to Helen. Escorting her to the dining room, they came to an abrupt halt at the appearance of two young boys bearing down on them. The boys reached Elliott and clamped their arms around him, one on each side. Elliott tousled their hair and grinned at Helen. "I'd like you to meet my sons, Harry and Tom."

Helen smiled a greeting. "How do you do?"

In unison, the two repeated her greeting.

Harry, the firstborn of the twins, was dark like his father. Tom was fair-haired like their mother, Helen noted, recalling the pictures in the parlor she'd seen of Elliott's pretty wife, Emily.

"All right, enough of the formalities," Elliott said. "Time to eat breakfast."

Helen was taken with the boys—until she lifted the silver cover off her breakfast plate. There sat a slimy grayish-green toad atop her eggs, staring up at her. She crashed the cover down on the plate.

Elliott stared at her in alarm. "Is something wrong?"

Darting a frown at each boy, she shrugged and serenely met his eyes. "Oh, my eggs aren't done quite the way I like them."

"Cook!" he shouted. "New eggs for Miss Jameson, please."

A sweet-looking gray-haired woman appeared in the doorway and wrung her hands. "Is something wrong with the eggs?" she asked, nodding at the covered plate.

"Oh, I'm really not all that hungry," Helen explained. "I ate before I left home."

Elliott nodded. "All right. As soon as I'm done, I'll take you on a tour of the house."

The house was three stories tall and exquisite. Helen loved it immediately. It was a Georgian-style. It was obvious that his wife, who'd adored her family and home, had resided here. Each room had been decorated with a loving hand.

All too soon Elliott was heading for the front door. He paused in the doorway and smiled at Helen. "You sure you'll be okay? I mean, I could try and get my housekeeper's daughter to help during the day with the boys."

She shrugged. Handling two little boys would be far easier than a classroom of fifteen students. "Don't worry," she said with a smile. "We'll be just fine."

He hugged Harry and Tom. Each boy clung to his legs and whined for him not to leave.

Helen saw through their protests, knowing well they were worried about how she'd deal with them for their breakfast prank after their father was gone. Still, she gave them a gentle smile. She'd lived through many such pranks with their father and George. Surely, she'd live through the next two weeks with these two just fine. But first, she planned to give them a taste of her own sweet revenge.

Elliott leaned down and kissed her cheek. "I'll send a telegram midweek."

Within twenty-four hours, Helen decided she'd made the biggest mistake of her life. Well…second biggest. Breaking off her engagement to Elliott took precedence. Perhaps if they'd married, their children would have been much less rambunctious. On second consideration of the boy Elliott himself had been, she didn't imagine a child of his could be any less mischievous and fun-loving.

On her third day in residence, Helen perused the boys' daily schedule which had been set up by the previous nanny. She decided they required more outdoor playtime than what was included on the list. She wasn't too long in the tooth to know how to toss and hit a ball. That was when the mishap—purely accidental—happened. She was pitching a ball to Harry. He'd smacked it with surprising force and the ball hit her in the eye before she had a chance to move or catch it. From there the day worsened, especially when the boys grew cranky at her insistence that they take a rest after the midday meal. They'd grudgingly retired to their room.

An hour later, she went to check on them, assuming they would be sleeping. She'd opened the door and her eyes widened in amazement at the disastrous condition of their room. Every toy was out and on the floor. They'd torn apart the covers off their beds and had been in the midst of a pillow fight. Just as she entered, one pillow sailed toward her. She put up an arm. The pillow hit it then burst open. Goose feathers swarmed the air. It had taken all afternoon to make them clean up the mess. She'd sat in a rocking chair and kept an eye on them the entire time, a towel filled with ice she held to her injured eye, which had turned black and blue, eventually encouraging them to finish or the day would be over, and it would then be bedtime. They moved more quickly then.

Thirteen days later, Elliott arrived home. The first words from his mouth made Helen's cheeks heat up. "What happened to you?" he said, aghast.

She knew she looked horrible with the remnants of the bruise-colored eye black, blue, and yellow. "Just a little mishap playing ball," she said.

"Thank God you weren't hurt," he murmured as he lightly touched the bruised skin around her eye. He gave her a gentle smile, and she forgot about the discomfort and smiled back.

Helen was glad he left it at that. After the past two weeks, she was ready for adult companionship. It was quite late when he'd arrived home. He'd insisted she stay the night, not a bit enamored of her traveling home in the late-night hours. Helen reluctantly agreed. Elliott was just too tempting to a schoolteacher spinster who'd only shared a few chaste kisses in her past, from him, her only beau.

While eating a late supper, Helen felt hot and frazzled from a day chasing after the boys. She set down her glass of wine and glared at Elliott. "Why didn't you tell me from the start that Harry and Tom are undisciplined little wretches?"

He shrugged off her accusation. "They're lively, fun-loving little boys, for sure."

"Fun-loving, you say?"

She saw the discomfort on his face. Lord, as much as she wanted to leave right this moment and never return, the look on his face told her she couldn't. He needed her.

Crash.

Helen darted a quick look up at the ceiling, then glanced at Elliott as he tossed down his napkin. "Excuse me."

He started striding from the dining room.

"Elliott?"

He paused, staring at her with one eyebrow quirked.

"Remember now, they're fun-loving boys," she said gently.

"Touché, my dear." His lips quirked in a parody of a smile before he rushed from the room.

Rubbing her temples, she heard him bounding up the stairs. Yes, they were just mischievous little boys, but she couldn't allow this unruly behavior to continue. In nearly two weeks' time, she'd suffered through more pranks than Elliott and George had ever played on her.

She left the table, meandering into the hallway to listen. All was quiet. In the parlor, she read the rest of the newspaper. An hour later, she quietly made her way up the stairs to check on the boys. Heavens, she hoped Elliott hadn't been too harsh on them.

The boys' bedroom door squeaked a bit as she pushed it open. One lamp was still lit. In the dimmed lighting, she saw that their two small beds had been pushed together. The boys lay with Elliott between them. His long legs hung off the bed's edge. He still wore his daytime attire with his shirt loosened and tie removed. His arm was around each boy, and they were snuggled one on either side of him. All three were sound asleep.

She smiled even as tears gathered in her eyes. She knew then that Elliott had spent many a night doing exactly this since his wife's death, and her heart ached at how stupid she'd been all those years ago. Ached because she'd been too stubborn and blinded by jealousy to believe him. How he'd ever forgiven her she couldn't say. But now, as she closed the door, she decided she'd be the best nanny he'd ever hired, and she'd stay the duration.

As Harry and Tom adjusted to Helen's rules, they grew to depend on her—and seemed to like her well enough. Five-year-old children could be so candid, she mused, thinking about Harry's hug this morning before he ran out the door to play in the yard. She'd gotten down on her knees, and he'd wound his arms around her neck and planted a sloppy kiss on her cheek.

Two months had passed, and while harmony in the household was sporadic but not unexpected with two five-year-old boys in residence, Helen was beginning to think of Elliott's home as her own. She spent far more time with Harry and Tom than with their father, which was unfortunate. Helen had found little time to renew her friendship with Elliott. And the few times she'd tentatively tried, he'd been polite but seemingly uninterested. She'd been hurt but knew she couldn't blame him. She'd shunned him before, so he didn't trust her. His reaction made her wonder why he wanted her to work for him and live in his household if it was too painful for him to have her there.

One Friday evening in November, Elliott arrived home late the third time that week. At the beginning of the week, he'd informed her he'd be late several evenings and asked her to stay overnight. She'd agreed, much too quickly, but then she was in love with the man, so what choice did she have?

And it seemed she didn't have to worry about her reputation. All of Elliott's and her mutual friends, family, and acquaintances had readily accepted the fact that she was caring for his sons just as the previous nannies who'd resided in his home. While shopping in town she'd heard no gossip—a great relief to her.

One evening, it was half past ten, and Helen was sitting in the parlor reading the newspaper when Elliott strode in. Brushing white stuff from his coat, he brought the cold with him. Her heart raced at the sight of him. She was glad she wore one of her finest day gowns, fashioned in midnight blue satin and embellished with lace on the collar and cuffs. He looked exhausted from the long hours he'd been working.

"Oh, it's snowing!" she exclaimed. She folded the newspaper and set it down on the table beside her.

He grumbled from the parlor doorway as he removed his overcoat, "Yes, and I hate it."

She smiled. "Oh, I remember when you loved it. Remember our snowball fights?"

He flashed her a grin. "Sure do. I'll be right back."

Soon he returned dressed in black pants that hugged his lean hips and long legs, a white starched shirt and black waistcoat. He'd removed his tie, and his shirt he'd loosened at the neck. He was handsome, strong, and virile. All she could think about was how she'd ruined things for herself by refusing to marry him. The lantern's glow caught the shiny silver chain holding his watch fob stuffed inside his pocket. His eyes twinkled with humor.

Her gaze followed him to the corner of the parlor, to a fine oak liquor cabinet. He poured two tiny glasses of sherry and returned to her side.

"Thank you." She sipped the sweet ruddy liquor.

They'd fallen into the habit of sharing a cordial the evenings he worked late. He claimed they both needed it to help them sleep. She agreed. The first few nights she'd stayed, she had difficulty falling asleep, knowing he was in his room down the opposite end of the hallway from her room. Though unsaid between them, Helen knew their feelings for each other would be kept at bay until George's debt had been paid.

He sank down on the divan beside her and tweaked one loose curl hanging over her shoulder. "About those snowball fights, if you'll remember, I always won."

"Not always," she smoothly replied, thinking it was mostly true. With his graceful athletic build, he was a natural at all endeavors of a physical nature. Suddenly, thoughts of the two of them sharing a bed entered her mind. *Physical endeavors, indeed!*

"Mostly," he replied.

She laughed. "You cheated often, you know."

"*Moi?*" he asked in mock indignation.

"Yes, you."

He shrugged. "Perhaps I was just smarter than the two of you."

She raised her brow. "I beg your pardon! Since when does cheating mean one is brilliant?"

"Intuitive then, not smarter."

"Now on that I can agree. You know, have you ever thought about changing occupations?"

He arched one eyebrow. "To what?"

"You would make an excellent spy for the government."

He chuckled. "Hmm, now that would be an interesting line of work, wouldn't it?"

"I've been meaning to ask how you came to own a steamboat."

"I won it."

"Ah, gambling then. You were very lucky," she said dryly.

"Yes, but I've been reformed, especially now that I see what the habit has done to others. Particularly, you and George."

"You mean you don't gamble any longer?"

"No, and I'm planning on selling *The Lucky Lady* soon. I'm away from home too much as it is with *The Sentinel* and the boys need me."

They sat side by side in silence before the small fire Helen had set in the hearth. She felt warm, cozy, and drowsy and soon started nodding off. She startled and opened her eyes at the sound of laughter.

"Come on, sleepyhead," Elliott said, rising from the divan. "Time for bed for both of us."

She gave him an astonished, round-eyed look.

"Oh, we are a pair, aren't we?" he said, laughing as he pulled her to her feet. Then he wound his arm around her shoulders and held her close. "I'm glad to see we're sharing the same thoughts. Soon, Helen, we'll be together."

She set her glass down, her hand shaking. "What?"

"You know of what I speak, so don't play coy with me. Once this damned debt between us has ended, I'll pursue you with a vengeance, you know."

Helen gulped, never having heard him quite so forceful before. Her body tingled at his words.

"Are you proposing marriage then?" she asked, her voice a mere whisper. Inwardly, she cringed at her daring. How could she even think to ask him such a question?

"Not yet, but soon. Come. I'll escort my lady to her boudoir."

Outside her door, she leaned against it, tilted her chin up, and met his eyes.

Oh, if he would only kiss her again, as a man kissed the woman he loved! But just small familial pecks had he given her since she'd begun working for him. Again, she found herself thinking about his words, *we were meant to be together*. She agreed.

She reached up and stroked a lock of dark hair off his forehead. Reaching out, he wound his fingers around her wrist. His grip moved down to her hand and he threaded his fingers through hers. Helen hugged the door and shivered at the intensity of his gaze. His nostrils flared as he drew closer to her lips, then he closed his eyes. Helen closed hers and hummed a sigh at his lips sealing hers.

He kissed her with such sweet longing, she couldn't help but wind her free arm around his neck. She stroked the nape of his neck and returned his kiss. She startled when he swept her up hard against his body, leaving her feet dangling above the floor.

Gladness soared through her. Tears filled her eyes then as he slowly released her and set her down on her feet. She opened her mouth to tell him she loved him when he saluted her, then said a quick "good night" and strode away. She watched him until he stopped at the end of the hallway; watched him open his door then pause to look back at her. She saw his satisfied smile just before he turned into his room and closed the door behind him.

December 1877

In two days' time, George's indebtedness would be paid in full. The three months had passed more quickly than Elliott had thought it would, especially since all he could think about was wooing Helen.

He'd wanted to pursue her ever since the death of his wife, but she wouldn't see him. George's gambling addiction had, ironically, brought them together again.

Elliott had nothing to lose and everything to gain by having Helen in his life again. He guessed, though, once he proposed to her, she'd accept because of the guilt she'd been harboring all these years for not believing he was a man of honor. He didn't want her guilt, only her love. Hopefully, once they married, she'd come to realize she loved him as much as he loved her. The last thing he wanted was guilt to be the only reason she had for accepting his proposal.

Elliott and George sat in the library at George's home, imbibing in brandy and conversation. "It isn't often I ask you to do something for me, George," Elliott said, "but I'm asking now. Will you watch the boys, so I can take your sister to the opera and dinner?"

George groaned. "You know I'd do just about anything for you, but not that. Please, not that."

"They're just five-year-old boys."

"True, but they're *your* boys. I vividly remember *you* as a boy. Frankly, I don't think I can handle their…spiritedness."

"You'll do fine. I'll make it worth your while."

Narrowing his eyes on his friend, George said, "How?"

"You may have *The Lucky Lady*."

George started coughing, spraying brandy from his mouth. His eyes watered when he looked at Elliott. "Now you tell me when I've already accepted a position at Andrews and Sons Law Firm."

Elliott shrugged. "So, you could have both, couldn't you?"

George scowled. "No. I promised my sister I'd stay away from *that* side of life from now on, and I meant it. Thanks anyway."

Grinning, Elliott said, "I believe you've learned your lesson, haven't you?"

"Absolutely."

"I plan on marrying your sister, if she'll have me."

"Well, what a surprise," George said without an ounce of said emotion. He laughed. "Have you asked her yet? And what do you mean *if* she'll have you. Of course she will! Like I said, she's loved you all this time."

Dryly, Elliott said, "You sound so sure of her when I'm not, though I'm beginning to think she still feels some tenderness in her heart for me. I just don't want her marrying me out of guilt."

"Ah," George said. "I understand, but I don't think you need to worry about that. I said it before, I'll say it again, she still loves you."

"I pray you're right."

Elliott had been frank with Helen, telling her they were meant to be together in blissful matrimony. He wouldn't allow her the opportunity to slip away as she'd done all those years ago.

"It's a deal," George said. "But could you have your housekeeper's daughter stay also? I may need some assistance with the boys."

Elliott rose with a smile. "Certainly."

George glared at Elliott's back as he headed out the door. "Where in hell are you off to in such a hurry?"

Elliott paused and turned with a gleam in his eye. "To ask your sister if I may call on her."

George shrugged. "Suit yourself, but you really don't have to rush off to do that now. Do you know it's almost ten? She's likely to be abed by now."

"I'm hoping she's waiting up for me."

"You know," George said casually, "she'll say yes."

Elliott raised his brow. "You know your sister so well?"

George nodded. "Like I said, she's been in love with you for years."

Elliott didn't discount Georgie's comment. He'd seen the joy in Helen's eyes several times since she'd come to work for him. Still, he wasn't ready to accept it—not from anyone but Helen herself. "I wonder about that."

"That's because Helen's always had that 'poker face.' Hell, she should have been the one gambling, not me."

Elliott laughed. "You're probably right."

Unfortunately, Helen was abed by the time Elliott arrived home. He vowed the very next day to begin courting her. The following morning, he woke to find the boys up but no sign of Helen. He soon learned from the cook she had a splitting headache and was resting in her bedroom. Elliott decided to spend the day at home with the boys instead of going to work. It had been ages since he'd taken any time off for himself and family. Then he'd be available if the boys needed anything. Who was he kidding? He'd be available if *Helen* needed anything.

It wasn't until late afternoon, when he and the boys came inside after frolicking in the snow, that he saw Helen descending the stairs. She held a hot water bottle against the side of her head. It was only then he recalled how she'd been prone to severe headaches in her youth.

He removed his coat, hung it in the closet before turning to assist Harry and Tom. She hadn't noticed them. Once she reached the bottom, she looked up and gasped. "Oh! You are all soaking wet! You must get out of those wet clothes. Go on upstairs and change into dry things before you catch your deaths."

"Can we have a fight tomorrow?" Tom asked eagerly, glancing at his father.

Elliott tousled the boy's blonde curls and grinned down at him, then at Harry. "Absolutely. I demand an opportunity to win, the sooner the better. Now, go on upstairs."

His gaze followed the boys as they ran up the stairs before he met Helen's wide-eyed gaze.

"When did you arrive home?" she asked.

"Last night. I arrived earlier than I'd thought, around ten-thirty or so, but you were already abed."

"Yes, my headache had started late afternoon."

"Is it any better?" he asked.

"A bit. It should be gone by tonight." She gave him a wry smile. "Don't you look cheery this morning?"

He drew closer. "Do you know what tomorrow is?"

"Why, Thursday, isn't it?"

Elliott laughed. "It is. And George's debt will be paid in full."

"Oh! So soon? How time flies, doesn't it?"

Elliott heard the sadness in her voice and smiled. Good. To his mind, her sadness meant she didn't want to leave him. "Surprisingly, it has," he said. "But that's because our time together has been so enjoyable, don't you agree?"

She nodded, and he caught the faint blush on her cheeks. His heart soared at the look in her eyes, one that appeared to say, *Yes, I'm ready to spend the rest of my life with you, Elliott.*

"I believe I'd told you of my intentions, once the debt was no longer between us. I've come-a-courtin'," he said. "How would you like to see *Don Giovanni* at the Regency Opera House with me on Saturday night?"

"Oh! That sounds wonderful, but I'm afraid I can't."

"Why not?" He frowned.

"What about the boys? Who will watch them?"

"I've made arrangements."

"You have?"

He nodded. "George has agreed to sit with them."

Helen smiled. "You're joking, of course."

"Not at all."

She started laughing.

"So, let me in on the joke," he said.

"George! Can you just see Harry and Tom with him? He's such a softy, they'll take great advantage of him, I'm afraid."

"He voiced his insecurity to me, so I told him we'd have my housekeeper's daughter stay as well."

"No! You won't call Mary." She gave him a satisfied smile. "I believe George is long overdue to have a taste of what *he* was like as a child."

He grinned. "Excellent point."

⚜

After their third outing, Elliott decided it was time to propose marriage. As Helen took a seat on the divan in her parlor, Elliott poured them each a sherry. He sank down beside her, tossed one arm over the sofa back, and leaned comfortably against her side. She snuggled beside him and they drank in companionable silence, watching the licking flames of the fire on the hearth he'd set upon their arrival home.

He gave Helen a sideways look as he set his glass down on the table at his elbow. He leaned forward, folded his hands, and stared into the fire as he tried formulating the flowery words of a marriage proposal.

Helen, mercifully, put him out of his misery. "Just say it," she cried.

Elliott heard the vehement tone in her voice and smiled wryly. "I love how you've always been so pragmatic. I adore how you don't expect all of the fancy words so many women do."

She shrugged. "Perhaps, when I was younger, it was important.

But I'm twenty-eight, Elliott, not twenty. Please, if you don't say the words, I'm very much afraid I'll embarrass myself and say them first."

He slid off the divan, then sank to one knee facing her. Her eyes rounded in surprise. "You didn't think I had it in me anymore, did you?" he drawled, a twinkle in his eyes.

"It's not necessary for you to—"

"Yes, it is."

Tears filled her eyes, and he groaned when one slid from the corner and down her cheek. "Oh, sweetheart, don't cry."

Obviously, it was the wrong thing to say for she sobbed in earnest now, covering her face with her hands. He kneeled there before her, feeling humbled, possessive. Feeling everything for this woman he loved for much of his life. He held her hands, stroked them, kissed them, waiting for her tears to subside. When they did, she astonished him as only Helen could. She slid off the divan and went down on both knees alongside him, her eyes shining bright, her hands clutching his.

He released one of her hands and dug in his waistcoat pocket. "Take this ring as a sign of my love and devotion. It represents the circle of unending love I've always felt for you." He slid the exquisite, perfectly round diamond on her finger then kissed her hand. She sniffled, and he dragged his gaze to hers.

"Please don't cry, darling. Just say yes," he said on a groan.

"If a woman can't cry after receiving the most exquisite marriage proposal of her life, when can she?"

Helen threw herself into his arms, nearly knocking him over. Laughing, he wound his arms around her waist, breathing in the sweet scent of her hair. Life couldn't be more perfect at this moment—with one exception. Saying the words between them and receiving God's blessing.

"I take it you accept?" he said, leaning back from her and gazing lovingly into her eyes.

"Yes!"

January 1878

Helen and Elliott's wedding day arrived amidst the biggest snowstorm Missouri had seen in years. When Helen stared out a window of a private room in St. Matthew's church, she realized she felt happy but calm and controlled—more than ready to marry the man she'd loved since her youth.

She looked down at her full-skirted satin taupe-colored gown, embellished with matching seed pearls and lace, and sighed. Never had she owned anything so beautiful and she wished she could wear it again but knew she wouldn't. This was the one and only time she planned on marrying.

Glancing at the handsome clock on the wall, she noted the time —twelve noon—then heard the church bells ring. Holding her head high, she plucked up her skirts and made her way to the church doorway where her friend, Renee, stood waiting for her, dressed in a cream-colored bridesmaid gown, her hands holding a small bouquet and a larger one, for Helen. Renee handed the bride her bouquet, then positioned herself behind Helen.

Her brother George stepped up to her side with a wide grin on his lips. When the music began, they made their way down the aisle, Renee following them past the pews decorated in flowers and lace. Helen's eyes were riveted on Elliott. He waited for her at the front of the church, his hands folded behind his back, his legs spread wide in a solid stance, his eyes focused only on hers.

They made their vows to each other, his in a strong voice, hers wavering, but firm.

After the ceremony, friends and family made their way to Elliott's home, which had been cleaned, the woodwork polished to a high sheen for the wedding reception. Every archway and doorway had been embellished with flowers, the large dining table as well had been decorated for their wedding feast. Elliott had had the table specially made and delivered to accommodate the forty guests they'd invited.

Helen sat at one end of the table, opposite her husband. She chatted with Renee on one side of her and Mrs. Pringle, owner of Brine's Bakery, who had supplied the luscious wedding cakes, on the other. The guests enjoyed a delicious meal consisting of hot cakes and maple syrup, boiled eggs, fried potatoes and biscuits and sausages, plus dainty fruit tartlets. There were three cakes also, in three flavors—almond, chocolate, and lemon.

Over the conversation of the guests, she heard the clock in the hallway chine four bells. She could hardly believe how quickly the day was passing, and already it was late afternoon. Frankly, she was exhausted after having risen early in the morning and was anxious for the festivities to end. Heat seeped into her cheeks as she thought about joining her husband in his bed. She sighed, wishing now she weren't a virgin. From her girlhood friends, she'd heard of the initial pain involved in making love for the first time. She felt excited and apprehensive at the same time.

By 7:00 p.m. she was so tired she was having difficulty keeping up with the conversation and her eyes open. A hand suddenly cupped her elbow. She smiled shyly at Elliott as he assisted her to her feet. Then he turned to their guests and said, "If you will excuse us, my dear wife needs her rest."

Her cheeks felt hot while she said her good-byes. Elliott escorted her from the dining room and up the stairs. They reached the second floor, and she said, "I should check on the boys, don't you think?"

"Of course," he said, giving her a slow smile. "I'll join you later, once I've seen our guests out."

Helen peeked into Harry and Tom's bedroom and smiled when she heard the even breathing of their sleep. Early to bed, early to rise, had been Helen's motto in life, but she admitted she was surprised by how early the boys had gone to sleep, especially with the reception happening downstairs. But they'd attended the wedding and had spent the earlier afternoon with playmates outdoors, and obviously had exhausted themselves.

Closing the bedroom door, she treaded softly down the hallway. She reached the guestroom, her room while she'd been the nanny, deciding to wait for Elliott there. They needed to talk this night— before sharing their wedding night in his bed.

Bending down from where she sat on the side of the bed, she removed her shoes and stockings then lay down, just to rest until Elliott arrived.

Within moments, he entered the room. Helen sat up, tossed her legs over the side of the bed, then froze in position when his gaze settled on her. She waited for Elliott to say—do—something. After a long while, after his eyes had taken in each and every curve of her body, he raised his eyes to hers. "You are the most beautiful woman I've ever seen, Helen Falconer. I feel blessed to be your husband, proud that you are my wife." He sank down to his knees in front of her.

"Elliott?" she said softly, catching his hands as they fluttered over her body. "Stop. We must talk."

He frowned. "This is our wedding night, albeit it is rather early to retire, but I find I can't wait any longer to have you."

She grew insistent. "No, truly, we should have talked about this the night you proposed to me."

Sighing, he said, "Now that we've married, none of what we feel or say will make a difference. Do you understand?"

"Yes, I do." She'd heard the steel in his voice and knew he'd never give her up, especially now that they were married. Her love for him grew even more because of it. She raised her eyes to him, knowing they held worry. "But I need to know, do you truly forgive me for having doubted you in the past? For having made your life miserable by breaking our engagement?"

He groaned and sank back on his heels as he stared up at her. "Doubting my intentions, doubting my love for you is hurtful, Helen. Do you know that? If I hadn't forgiven you, I wouldn't have asked you to marry me. Now it's my turn. Did you marry me because of deep-seated guilt because of the past or because you love me?"

Haltingly, she replied, "Initially, when we first met again, I have to admit guilt played a part. But, once I'd started working for you those feelings subsided, mostly because I began to believe you'd gotten your just revenge by placing me in charge of your two mischievous sons. But then I soon fell in love with them. I love you, Elliott. I always have."

Love and desire blazed in his eyes. She saw it, believed it—believed in him.

"So, are we through talking?" he asked.

She nodded.

He swept an intimate look over her bodice. "Come, it's time to retire…in *my* bed."

She rose then, reaching down and pulling him up to his feet. They made their way to his room.

Once inside, Helen daringly reached up and started unbuttoning his fine white shirt. He impatiently finished undressing himself, and her, then pulled her down to the bed and lay down beside her. His hands cupped her breasts, and she groaned. His kisses promised unknown but wildly anticipated pleasure. She couldn't get enough of them.

Then and there she decided he *must* love her—must have forgiven her. He took such great care to bring her joy and pleasure that she felt only a momentary twinge of pain when he joined with her. He made love to her twice more during the night, and Helen realized if he'd asked it of her, she would have joyously done so again a third time. They entered into an exhausted sleep in each other's arms.

She felt his hands on her early the next morning. Rolling to face him, she smiled. She kissed the pulse beating in his neck and breathed in the wonderful male scent of him.

"Mine," she heard him murmur. "Finally."

Her heart nearly burst with gladness. My God, he loved her. He truly loved her.

She pulled back from him to give him an impish smile. "For always?" she breathed, her eyes misting over tearfully again.

"Always, Helen."

New Orleans, June 1878

Elliott headed toward Helen, where she leaned against the railing of *The Lucky Lady*, a flute of champagne in each hand. Upon George's refusing the offer of the steamboat, Elliott had decided to keep it after all, hiring a capable captain for it. It was a solid investment for him, used mainly for passenger travel and some cargo hauling as it made trips up and down the Mississippi River.

Finally, five months after marrying, they went on their honeymoon. Arrangements for someone to care for the boys had to be made, and his business affairs taken care of, in order for them to have this month together. Now the honeymoon was nearly over, and they would be returning home within the week.

"Here, sweetheart," Elliott murmured as he handed her a flute. "To us," he said, tapping his glass against hers. "Yes," she said softly, then drank along with him.

Sinking against the railing, elbow to elbow, they were both quiet as they looked out at the river. Lights from the city of Minneapolis reflected off the water. They'd decided to enjoy the month of June up north, leaving the heat and humidity of Missouri behind them. The weather had been lovely thus far and they'd basked in it, taking tours of each city they traveled through as they headed north, relaxing on the steamboat's deck in the evening after supper.

"Oh!"

Elliott startled at the sound of his wife's singular utter. "What is it, sweetheart?" he asked, sliding an arm around her waist and pulling her against him.

"Why, look at the dancing lights," she exclaimed, "and the colors!"

He followed the direction of her eyes and frowned. "Dancing lights? The only lights I see are from the city."

"No, no, look above the city lights, into the sky where it's darker. Do you see them?"

He tipped his head back a bit further, watching, then gasped. "I can't believe it. I've read about the Aurora Borealis, but never imagined seeing them in my lifetime."

"I've read about them," Helen said, "in a science book in your library. I just never imagined seeing them either." She grinned at him, pulled up onto her toes, and kissed his cheek. "How lucky we are, and so blessed."

His grin deepened. "You are so right. We have a wonderful life together, don't we?"

She nodded, and he caught the dimple in her cheek and the mischievous sparkle in her eyes. "What?" he asked in a dubious tone.

"Nothing," she said slowly, shrugging her shoulders and nestling even closer against him. He looked at her, puzzled, when she took his hand and settled it against her middle. "Well, something…" she added softly.

He looked at her for the longest time, her brows arched above her lovely eyes, then knew. "Are you…"

"Yes," she said quickly.

"Are you sure?" He pulled her to face him and wound his arms tightly around her, holding her flush against his body.

"Yes, and so very happy." He caught the hesitant look in her eyes as she bit her lower lip, then said, "I hope you're as happy about this as I am."

Elliott's eyes filled with tears; Helen was going to have their child and he couldn't be happier. Now he understood why she'd been sick for that month before they left on their honeymoon.

"Ecstatic. You are the wonder of my life, Helen. I welcome any children you give me—a houseful of them. As a matter of fact, I've always wanted my own baseball team."

She frowned. "But what if we have all daughters?"

"Girls can play baseball," he said with a sure nod. "Just you watch."

THE END

TO LOVE A MUSIC MASTER

Piano virtuoso, Jasper Hughes, once found his piano student Annabelle Watkins undisciplined. Seven years have passed since their tumultuous parting. Now she's back on his doorstep, asking Hughes to teach her again. He reluctantly agrees, and finds himself falling in love with her, and she with him.

November 1890, New York City

A nnabelle Watkins stood outside the Hughes School of Music, a pristine, white-gloved hand poised and ready to knock on the door. The prestigious school, housed in an old brownstone building, was located on the corner of Fifth and Cedar. Annabelle was personally familiar with the school.

Covertly, she glanced around, knowing she should not have left her chaperone behind. Society frowned upon unmarried women of an available age gallivanting (as her mama used to say) alone about town. However, it was daylight and she was twenty-two years old, not some young girl directly out of the schoolroom. Recently, Annabelle concluded that her prospects at finding a suitable beau were diminishing with the passing of time, resigning herself to the possibility of subsiding into a sorry state of spinsterhood for the rest of her life. The thought brought tears to her eyes and she choked back a sob.

Annabelle straightened her peacock-blue hat and brushed a piece of lint off her matching woolen coat. Tucking one strand of wheat-colored hair into her new coiffure, a loosened bun atop her head, she knocked briskly on the door, and then backed down one step. The worst that could happen was that Master Hughes could simply tell her "no," he wouldn't take her as a student again.

Annabelle supposed she couldn't blame him if he declined, thinking of their past history. Embarrassment swept through her as she thought about her final momentous lesson with Hughes several years ago; it had not been pretty, albeit it had been memorable. Her words at the time had rung out, loud and clear, laced with sarcasm that she would never step foot inside his studio again. Now here she was, with little choice in the matter.

The door swung open, heat escaping with it. Annabelle welcomed the warmth and was eager to enter—until she met the glaring expression of one of the world's most talented pianists. Master Jasper Hughes stood slim and tall, hair unfashionably long and bronze-colored, flowing to his shoulders, eyes a perfect shade of robin's egg blue. Attired head to toe in black, his hair was a stark contrast. Undeniably handsome, he was also, in Annabelle's memory, a harsh taskmaster who expected nothing less than perfection from his students.

Seven years had not changed him much, and she found her heart beating a bit faster as she viewed his handsome face. She'd been in love with him all those years ago and wondered at her heart's palpitations now upon seeing him again.

The man had been grouchy, and unsmiling, and still, she found herself falling in love with him. She had hoped, with the passage of time, to fall out of love with him, but now knew she hadn't, which was a problem. All she wanted from him were piano lessons, nothing else. And she was a woman full-grown, not a fifteen-year-old schoolgirl. With a nod, she squared her shoulders and met his scowling visage.

His scowl softened somewhat as he looked down at her. "Well, what is it?" he said rather impatiently. "I'm with a student."

"I…well, I…"

"Spit it out, young woman," he snapped. Then he narrowed his eyes on her until she noted how they darkened, and a humorless smile crossed his lips. She realized then he recognized her, and she braced herself for what she decided would be some form of chastisement. He'd been excellent at dressing her down when she was his student.

"Well, well, if it isn't Miss Annabelle Watkins, in the flesh."

She heard the irony in his voice but forced a smile on her lips. "Not quite," she said, knowing well how he had always hated her contrariness. Still, she could not help but taunt him. "I am wearing a simple day dress under my coat, and—"

The teacher swept her body a disdainful look. "I could care less what you are wearing. You could be standing there without a stitch and I would not care. I must return to my student. Good day, Miss Watkins."

Annabelle snatched up her skirts, moved up to the stoop to stand behind him. "But you have no idea why I've come!"

He paused in shutting the door, turned, and lifted his brow. "I could have sworn I'd said I don't care."

Annabelle jammed her black kid boot in the doorway, preventing him from closing the door, for once in her life satisfied with the rather large size of her foot.

He looked down with a sigh, then up, glaring at her. She imagined that at any moment she would see smoke seeping from his ears and eyes. The thought nearly caused her to laugh aloud, but that would not bode well for her at all. From experience, she knew that Mr. Hughes possessed little sense of humor. Rarely had she seen him so much as crack a tiny smile.

"You left seven years ago. You said you were through taking

lessons from me. In fact, I distinctly recall you telling me to go to Hades. Now remove your foot." Then, as an afterthought, he added, "Please."

She kept her foot right where it was. "I will wait here until you're through with your student. I must speak with you about resuming lessons."

"In what?" he snapped, "Proper behavior?"

Annabelle gasped, then said, "I beg your pardon. Why, I never misbehaved as your student!"

He rolled his eyes heavenward. "Heaven help me. Never could I have imagined such a day would arrive. You're right, of course, until that final day when you had your say, you had been well-behaved, yet lazy about practicing. Stay, if you must." Master Hughes grabbed her arm and pulled her inside, slamming the door behind them.

She stifled her shriek of surprise. "What in heaven's name are you doing?"

"I can't very well leave you standing in the hallway, can I?" He led the way into the parlor, which she knew was next to the music room. There, she took a seat in a chair positioned in front of a blazing fire, grateful for the warmth.

He turned to leave her but paused when she gasped at the sight of two huge dogs rising from their bookend places by the hearth.

"Stay there. I will be done shortly," he ordered.

Her hackles rose. Had he been talking to her or his dogs? She stood up and gave him a brisk salute. "Yes, sir! But aren't you taking them with you?" Annabelle pointed at the dogs, now seated and watchful.

"Still the comedienne, are you?" he said dryly.

"No one has ever accused me of not having a sense of humor."

He shrugged off her comment. "Roscoe and Rufus will keep you company." He started to leave but paused then and swept his gaze over her body. "You may want to remove your coat. The fire will roast you, otherwise."

Her gaze followed Master Hughes, one of the most handsome men she'd ever known, as he left the parlor. After he disappeared into his music room, she turned to stare into the fire. His watchdogs would be watching over her so that she couldn't change her mind and leave. Annabelle stood, ready to pace the floor, when the dogs rose in unison and growled.

She gasped, then sank down in her chair, rearranged her small bustle before leaning back, her gaze on the dogs that had settled down again, closing their eyes. Annabelle guessed they weren't sleeping at all but sensing her every move. She shrugged off her coat and tried to relax, listening to the music from the adjacent room. The student was gifted for not a single note did he or she miss.

Annabelle watched the leaping flames for a while then checked the delicate gold watch pinned to her bodice. It was after four, and she must arrive home by five before her father, or else he would worry. He didn't want her "traipsing about," as he called it, after dark. With the coming of December, the days had grown ever shorter and darkness came earlier and earlier.

Her eyes fluttered against her cheeks and she sighed as she slumped low in the high-backed, comfortable chair. Sometime later, feeling wonderfully warm, she woke with a start and sat straight up in her chair. The fire had dwindled, and she heard nothing but the ticking clock on the wall.

She rubbed her sleepy eyes and glanced around the parlor, disoriented, gasping at the sight of Master Hughes sitting on the divan across from her. He appeared relaxed and calm, but wore an intense look in his eyes, his dogs at his knees. She had fallen asleep and her cheeks heated in embarrassment, thinking he'd been staring at her.

"You have turned into a beautiful woman, Miss Watkins."

His voice was cool and low, tinged with cynicism, as though he resented the fact she'd grown up.

"I'd bet my last half dollar you cause your good father more than a hint a worry in life, don't you?" He raised his brows. "Or have you a husband and his worry now?"

Annabelle chose not to take umbrage with his personal comments. "No husband and thank you for the compliment. I think."

He laughed aloud as he rose to his feet and stuck out his hand to assist her. Annabelle sat stock-still, stunned by his smile and laughter. There went her heart again, racing. Finally, she placed her hand in his and he pulled her up. With her free hand, she picked up her coat and carried it over her arm. Hughes tucked her arm through his, guiding her into the music room. There he released her and waved at the piano bench.

"Sit. Play. I'd like to hear where I left off with you all those years ago."

Annabelle stayed far away from the piano and clutched her hands together. "Um, that's why I'm here. I believe I've forgotten everything you taught me."

Jasper groaned and waved a negligent hand to a side chair nearby. She moved to the chair and took a seat, straightening her skirts and not meeting his eyes. Amanda glanced up and saw him striding toward the piano. Sinking down on the bench, he sat facing her rather than the piano and clasped his hands in front of him. "Tell me why you require my services."

That was blunt, Annabelle decided, and it was much to her liking since she had no time for dilly-dallying. "Months ago, my father asked me to learn to play several pieces of music, in order to entertain guests from Great Britain coming to visit us over the holidays. As you well know, Christmas is only five weeks away and—"

"Months ago, you said." He raised his brow. "Had you begun attempting to learn the pieces on your own?"

"I am certain you recall my penchant for procrastination."

"Unfortunately, yes. It's the only reason why I could no longer instruct you. You refused to practice between lessons." Sweeping a disdainful look at her, he dryly added, "It seems you have not changed as much as I believed after all."

Annabelle's cheeks grew hot at his accusation, wanting to tell him how wrong he was about her, yet she refused to defend herself —refused to tell him how she had struggled with the music from the day her father had asked her to prepare to play for his guests.

Over the past several months, she'd gone from teacher to teacher, but no one had been able to help her. Frankly, she was a dunderheaded female when it came to learning music, and playing the piano, though her father thought her talented. Of course, he knew nothing at all about music. Let Master Hughes think the worst of her. She did not care. As long as he took her on as a student, she'd have somewhat of a chance learning the pieces. The only procrastination she'd done was delaying coming to him for help.

"Think what you like," she said crisply.

"Correct me if I'm wrong, or is your head still in the clouds over some boy?"

"Man, you mean. I am, after all, a woman full grown."

His piercing, long look made her straighten her spine. Amanda watched in amazement—for the music master had always been so impersonal—sweep his gaze from her head to her feet. Softly, she heard him say, "Yes. You certainly are that."

ॐ 2 ॐ

S haking himself out of his stupor, Jasper was disgusted with himself and his attraction to this woman whom he'd always believed was too shallow, too societal for his tastes, and unfortunately, too easy on the eyes.

Seven years ago, she had also been too young, yet even back then, he couldn't deny his attraction for her. Looking at Miss Watkins, he couldn't deny how she'd grown into an exceptional beauty. He'd noticed her smooth carriage from the moment he had dragged her into his house. He also noticed how her young, girlish shape had swelled into womanly curves as he admired her in her russet-colored day gown. Her thick hair the color of wheat she wore pinned up beneath a small woolen hat.

"That's all you have to say then? You admit you procrastinated?" he snapped.

"Yes. "She raised her brow. "Why are you in such a snit over it, might I ask?"

"Because nothing has changed," he growled as he rose to his feet. Pacing, he lectured her. "You cannot expect to become a decent musician if you procrastinate in practicing. Why should I waste my time on you?" He planted his hands on his hips and scowled down at her in his most intimidating manner. "Why?"

She didn't answer his question but said, instead, "I'll double your normal fee."

"Do you think I teach because of the money? I earn a pittance from the lessons. I don't need money. I've inherited enough for ten lifetimes," he snarled, sinking to the piano bench once more, facing the piano this time.

He started playing a tune, loudly, with growing impatience and fury. By the time he finished he turned and found his guest cringing with her hands over her ears. He was sweating, adrenaline flowing, and he felt ready to play again harsh, pounding music to remove the woman from his mind. If he didn't, he decided he would either kiss her or toss her over his knee for some much-deserved punishment. Then pain suddenly shot through his wrist and hand and he knew he had strained himself, derisively recalling the illness preventing him from playing professionally.

"Leave," he ordered. He set his hands to the keys once more but played in a tame, easy manner now. When he finished the song, he rose from the bench and turned, surprised to see Annabelle sitting there still. She'd closed her eyes and tears ran down her fair cheeks. His heart clenched at the sight, but he kept his expression bland.

"Why haven't you left?" he asked, his voice filled with exhaustion.

Her eyes opened, and he saw the pain in them. He cursed himself then as he felt his heart thumping madly for her and knew that he had no choice but to teach her again. It would be torment for him because he wouldn't be able to touch her, still he knew he'd do it. He had to—for her—even though she didn't deserve him to, even though he knew it would be a waste of his valuable time.

He'd had plenty of regrets when she left all those years ago—
he had, in fact, taken her desertion personally—even if his
impatience had driven her away.

"I can't. You must help me."

He heaved a sigh. "Once again, I ask, what good reason have
you for procrastinating and not following your father's wishes to
begin earlier?"

"My father will be disappointed if I don't learn to play. He has
always wanted me to be like my mother. He still hasn't come to
terms with the fact that I'm not like her. I am who I am. Still, he's
asked this of me and—"

Jasper heard her shaking voice, heard her pause. Yes, her
mother had been musically gifted, and anyone would have had
difficulty following in the woman's footsteps.

He noticed how Annabelle wouldn't meet his eyes but stared
down at her hands. "And?" he asked.

Lifting her chin, she met his gaze. He saw the tears there still.
Groaning inwardly, he thought, Lord, keep me from taking her into
my arms and offering her comfort. She is nothing but a willful
society woman with little brains in her head. And she's been in my
thoughts all these years.

"I don't want to embarrass my father in front of his guests."

"Or yourself?" he insinuated.

She didn't reply at first, but instead gave him a long thoughtful
look. He knew her answer even before she replied. Jasper's heart
soared with hope that she had changed—that she was not still the
shallow young woman he once knew.

"Why, I hadn't thought about myself at all."

Jasper sank back against the piano, hitting keys with his
elbows. After a long moment staring at her, enjoying the pretty
picture she made, he rose, escorted her to the door, one arm around
her waist, the scent of her intoxicating. "Here are the lesson times

and conditions. I'll give you a lesson three times a week, Mondays, Wednesdays and Fridays for two-hour sittings for the next three weeks. You will practice, at the minimum, two hours each day after you take your lesson."

"Oh!" She stopped in the hallway, frowning. "I can't possibly make that sort of lesson commitment. You likely won't believe this but there are other things to do in life aside from playing the piano."

"For instance?" he asked mildly, keeping his temper in check as he strode ahead of her and opened the front door.

She rushed up to him. "Paying calls to friends, for one. With the holidays approaching, I have many social engagements to attend."

He jammed his hands on his hips. "Once again, I state, you have not changed one bit, have you? Do you know you are still a shallow excuse for a human being?" Jasper noted the quick flash of anger mixed with tears in her eyes, and immediately regretted his crass words.

"And you are horrible as ever!" Annabelle drew herself up straight and tall, and glared at him in return.

"That is nothing I haven't heard before," he said dryly. "Those are my terms. We've much ground to cover between now and Christmas. Be ready to work like you've never worked before."

She stepped outside and looked at him over her shoulder. "And if I choose not to abide by this unreasonable schedule?"

"Then I'm afraid I can't help you," he replied with little inflection. "Good day, Miss Watkins."

With a finality he felt deep inside, guessing she wouldn't be returning, hard taskmaster that he was, he closed the door on her, leaned back against it until he heard her footsteps fade away.

On the ride home, Annabelle clenched her jaw and fisted her hands in her lap. Shallow? How dare the man! He knew nothing about her or her charity works; knew nothing about her work at the hospital. Why hadn't she told him about her good deeds instead of using the excuse of being a social butterfly? She knew the answer; it was difficult talking about her good deeds without feeling boastful. Pride was a sin, in her opinion.

Gathering her courage, she decided she would have to inform her father that she wouldn't be able to entertain his guests and that there was still time to hire a professional musician. Wryly, she thought, since Master Hughes was so critical of her, perhaps her father could pay him to perform.

She arrived home quarter of an hour before her father and was helping Cook serve up supper—a chore she knew, as the lady of the house she shouldn't do—but she loved cooking. As she bustled around the kitchen, following Cook's instructions, she heard the front door open and knew her father had arrived.

Arthur Watkins was a tall, distinguished, gray-haired man in his early sixties and was prone to frowning—not in anger but in concentration. He was calm and gentle, and as Ambassador to Great Britain, he was a logical, analytical peacemaker, and a true diplomat.

Annabelle had always been proud of him, though he hadn't always demonstrated his pride in her. Before her mother died, he'd doted on his wife and daughter. Things had changed between him and Annabelle with her mother's death. Her father had wanted her to be like her mother, but had learned, with some disappointment, she would never be like Grace Watkins, in appearance or temperament.

Arthur seated Annabelle and then took his own seat with a rare smile. "How was your day, dear?" he asked her.

Annabelle smiled. "Wonderful. Remember the two children

who'd been burned in the tenement fire down on Cook Street?" At his nod she added, "They've been released from the hospital."

"That's a good thing, though I have to say their lives will never be the same, will they?"

She shook her head sadly. "No. Unfortunately they'll live their lives as scarred individuals, inside and out."

After a few moments of small talk, Annabelle tensed up guessing the direction the conversation would be turning. As they sat back in their chairs and drank coffee after finishing their meal, Arthur smiled. "How is the music coming along?"

"Well...it's coming along...marvelously." Biting her lip, she wished she could be truthful. Why couldn't she just tell him that she was incapable of learning Mozart, Chopin, and Beethoven? Oh, she could play popular music just fine but the famous musicians— no, the music was too difficult and beyond her ability to learn.

Leaning forward in his chair, he placed his elbows on the table and smiled at her. "I am so proud of you for taking up the piano again, and I'm looking forward to hearing you entertain my guests." He tossed down his linen napkin then and rose from the table. "Are you finished?"

She stumbled to her feet. "Yes, I...I believe I'll retire early tonight." She gave him a small smile. "I may possibly be taking a lesson or two with Master Hughes."

"Hughes?" Her father arched one eyebrow. "Your old teacher? Why, you detested the man." He paused. "Come to think of it, you detested each other, as I recall."

"No, I didn't hate him, just the lessons."

He frowned. "But you don't now?"

"No, I believe I'll enjoy taking instruction from him again," she said. "I've grown up, I suspect, and I have become more disciplined."

"You've made a decision to return to him then?"

"Yes."

"He's an excellent teacher, His reputation is fine and his talent unmatched by none. Truthfully, Annabelle, I've no idea why you left him all those years ago. Think of how good a pianist you'd be now if you'd stuck with the lessons."

Her father cinched things for resuming lessons from Jasper Hughes when he said, "Your mother would be so happy if she were here. You know that, don't you?"

"Yes," she said softly, "I know she would." Annabelle swallowed down the lump in her throat—the one that was always there at the mention of her mother.

In her bedroom that night, she made a mental list of both the good and the bad things about taking lessons from Master Hughes, and in the end decided that the good outweighed the bad.

She would learn to play for her father's guests. She would not disappoint him. Annabelle would show Master Hughes, prove to him tomorrow that she could learn to play, and she would be the best student he had ever had. She'd sacrifice her charity work to spend the time on lessons and practice, to save her father humiliation, and to please him.

She knew she would succeed, for no one could ever accuse Annabelle of being less than tenacious when she desired something.

❦

Jasper was teaching a lesson the following morning to a talented fourteen-year-old boy named Riley Beacham when he heard rapping on his door.

"Continue playing, Riley." Irritation flooded him as he strode down the hallway, massaging his right hand, which had gone numb and lifeless after demonstrating a particularly difficult passage for

Riley. A deep melancholy feeling settled inside of him as he thought about his afflictions from the disease—one doctors were unable to diagnose.

Reaching the door and hating the interruption, he was eager to return to Riley, whom he so thoroughly enjoyed teaching. He couldn't hide the surprise on his face when he opened the door to Annabelle Watkins. There she stood, looking even more beautiful, if possible, than the day before. He hadn't expected her to return. Tongue-tied, he stared at her, waiting for her to speak first.

Raising one finely arched eyebrow she murmured, "I see you still don't believe in household help, do you?"

"I enjoy my privacy and am perfectly capable of answering my own door."

"And do you do your own cooking as well?"

Jasper nearly laughed outright at her audacious comment. "No. Cook comes in each morning and prepares my meals for the day. And I have a housekeeper who runs a broom through the place upon occasion." His smile slipped when he added, "None of them reside here, though."

He'd never wanted household help living with him, recalling how they'd gossiped about his parents during their marriage and the pain he'd suffered as a young boy after his father divorced his mother for infidelity.

As he escorted Annabelle into the parlor, he had difficulty reconciling this woman to the girl he taught years ago. She'd grown into a confident, vital, beautiful woman, though she had been a shy girl when he first knew her—until he'd made the mistake of correcting her in a rather unkind manner. In hindsight, he knew he'd been unjust toward her, realizing he'd behaved this way in order to fight his growing, amorous feelings for her.

Recalling that final day after her lesson, Annabelle had grown so angry with him that she'd thrown her music book at him. He'd been furious with her for she would never practice between their lessons, which hindered her progress. After a horrendous argument between them, she'd stormed from his house, never to be seen again. He wondered if she'd be that impetuous now that she was grown.

Annabelle took a chair in the parlor again but looked around cautiously.

"No need to worry. The dogs are outside." He glanced at his pocket watch. "I'll be done in ten minutes. Then we'll talk. There's tea on the table, if you like."

Half an hour later, Jasper knew he wouldn't be able to teach her well enough to play in public, at least not the music her father had requested she learn. Her beautiful, long, tapered fingers were wasted on her since she did nothing but stumble over the keys with them. She played fairly well with each hand, separately, but she was unable to put the two together. Jasper ended up doing the only thing he could do; he started from the beginning, as he would if he were teaching a young child. Surprisingly, he managed to maintain patience.

"All right, Miss Watkins, enough for today," he said after two long hours of torture. The poor woman appeared exhausted.

On shaky legs, she rose to her feet and quietly said, "Excuse me. Your…your, um…"

"The necessary room is near the back door, at the end of the kitchen," he gently informed her. "Remember?"

Upon her return, she picked up her reticule and music book. With a smile, she reached out and took his hand, surprising him. But as they clasped hands his heart raced at the warmth, and he had no desire to release her.

"Thank you for trying your best to teach me. I know now it's an impossible task, so I won't bother you further with your time. How much do I owe you?"

He frowned and made his gaze severe. He couldn't allow her to walk out his door—again. "We're not through yet, Miss Watkins."

"I'm afraid we are." She pulled her hand from his, turned, and headed for the door, pausing at his words.

"So, just like that, you're giving up?"

"Just like that," she said with her back to him. "Please invoice me and I will pay you promptly."

"I never considered you would give up so soon."

She bit her lip a moment then replied, "Hadn't I all those years ago?"

"You were a young girl with other things on your mind," he reminded her.

She whirled around and faced him, her smile widening. "True. But you can't deny I'm a hopeless case and will never learn to play Chopin."

"No, I don't know that," he said as he moved to her side. Lord, but what a smile! He couldn't allow her to leave without getting a further lesson commitment from her. "After one lesson, you can't give up."

"I've had several lessons with other teachers and didn't improve."

"They hadn't a clue how to teach you. Give this some time, at least another few lessons." Why was he trying so hard to convince her to stay? There was no denying that she was an abysmal pianist, but he'd be damned if he was going to give up on her. Call it ego or pride, but there had never been a student that he could not teach. Liar! You want her near you because you want her for your own.

"Why are you being so patient, so kind to me?"

He saw the wonder on her face, heard it in her voice. Straightening his jacket, he said, "Because I believe you have hidden talent, and that you can learn to play. Besides, my integrity is at stake here, you know. Do you think I want it bantered about town that I'd failed in teaching you?" *Not to mention the fact now that I've seen you again, I want nothing more than to take you to my bed and make love to you.*

"I promise not to say a word to anyone," she murmured.

He couldn't allow her to walk out that door without convincing her to return. If she left, he knew he never would see her again. Generally, the only women who interested him were unhappily married ones—safe ones not looking for a husband, but just some love and attention in their lives. Since surviving his parents' disastrous marriage as a young boy, he'd long ago decided never to commit to one woman—never to marry. The married state was filled with too much angst, jealousy, lack of trust, and heartache for a human being to have to live through. Besides, he didn't believe it was human nature for people to stay in love with only one person for a lifetime.

For the first time he was uncertain about his past thoughts in the matter. Another knock on the door drew him out of his reveries. His face burned when he saw Annabelle looking at him, studying him, trying to delve beneath his surface.

"I've another student," he said abruptly.

"Of course you do." She stepped aside allowing him to open the door for both her and his next student. Millie Hawkins, the daughter of the Ambassador to Germany, stood on the doorstep, with a chaperone behind her.

"Why, Millie, good to see you," Annabelle said.

Millie nodded, her blue eyes merry and mischievous.

3

J asper steeled himself to teach the young woman, not an easy task since she would usually spend much of her time during her hour-long lessons batting her long eyelashes at him. She was nineteen years old, just a few years younger than Annabelle, and utterly beautiful. She'd also, to his chagrin, rather blatantly settled her attentions on him, instead of moving in her typical social circles to find a husband.

He'd done everything he could, aside from being outright nasty, to curtail her flirtations and interest, but nothing had worked. Even with her chaperone sitting in the music room with them, Miss Hawkins flirted with him outrageously. A thought came to him then, and he waited for the right moment to plead his case to Annabelle.

Millie glared at Annabelle. "I hadn't realized you'd taken up piano again."

Annabelle replied, "Yes, well, I never realized you were a pianist."

"Oh, I'm not, but Master Hughes is being ever so helpful."

"Why begin lessons now at such a vast age?"

Jasper covered his smile behind a hand, silently approving of Annabelle's pragmatism. His smile broadened, and he pulled his hand away from his mouth. Annabelle was jealous of Millie!

Millie sniffed. "To answer your rather rude question, Master Hughes believes I have some talent.

Leaning back against the doorjamb, Jasper settled in to watch with interest the exchange between the two women. Then he groaned inside at the simpering look Millie gave him as she took his arm.

"Excuse me. I must take my lesson in a timely fashion as I've shopping to do afterward."

"Of course you do," Annabelle said coolly.

Jasper looked at Annabelle. "Why not join us for a bit? Perhaps once you hear what I've been able to teach Miss Hawkins, you'll have more confidence in me as a teacher."

Annabelle gave him a curious look, and if he wasn't mistaken, she was reading the hopeful look in his eyes that said, *Stay! Save me from this little twit!*

"Excellent idea," Annabelle replied.

Millie spoke up. "Oh! I cannot take a lesson with her standing by, Master Hughes."

"Of course you can, my dear. Miss Watkins won't be critical, and you may be able to teach her something she has yet to learn."

That gave her pause and she smiled. "True. Absolutely true."

❧

It was pure torture listening to Millie play. The woman played worse than Annabelle, if that was possible. Her chaperone sat in a corner chaise, knitting away, likely to put the music out of her head.

Poor Master Hughes had sunk deep into a chair beside

Annabelle, his head in one hand and the other moving as though he was directing a concert along with Millie's mistake-ridden playing, counting one-two-three in an effort to keep her on her timing.

At the end of the piece, Annabelle rose from her seat and clapped her hands. "Thank you for that, Millie. But now I really must be leaving." She turned to Master Hughes.

He scowled up at her from his reclining position. Annabelle nearly laughed outright, for his facial expression seemed to say, *how dare you leave me alone with this horror!* He rose slowly to his feet and inclined his head. "I'll see you day after tomorrow then, Miss Watkins?"

Ah, he'd thrown the challenge at her and waited now to see how she would respond.

Drawing herself up, Annabelle said, "You most certainly will. Good day to both of you."

Annabelle climbed into her waiting carriage and settled in.

Upon her arrival at Master Hughes' school, snow had begun to fall, and now a thick white blanket of it clung to the grounds and foliage. The temperatures had plummeted, and she huddled inside her coat, her hands tucked into her pockets. The humor of the situation she'd just observed caused her to smile and then to laugh outright as she recalled Hughes' pained expression while Millie played. She thought about Master Hughes' challenging comments, too, but she wouldn't immediately rise to the bait. She had much to think about, and she would not allow his comments to sway her own mind.

Jasper Hughes hadn't changed much, she decided, with the exception of a bit of premature graying at his temples. He was a man in prime physical condition. He wore his bronze-colored hair long—same as he had done years ago, making her wonder why he hadn't succumbed to the day's current fashion where men wore their hair short. She knew the answer. Hughes hated society's rules and avoided them at all costs, with one exception—guarding his reputation as a music master. He was his own man who lived his life according to his own rules and no one else's. She had admitted, even as a fifteen-year-old, that she had admired him for his individuality, and she was glad he had not changed.

She thought about the holiday festivities soon to take place and toyed with the thought of inviting him to her home. But then, she mused, being so famous, he likely would receive several invitations other than hers. Even though he'd been forced to stop performing years ago, he was a renowned musician and New York society loved him. No, she was certain he wouldn't have time to attend a party at her home, but it couldn't hurt to send him an invitation.

❧

Annabelle fought with herself the entire next day. Should she or shouldn't she return to Master Hughes on the morrow? She'd only told him she would to spite Milly. But now, in her own home, her sensible nature came to the fore.

Finally, with the thought that the holidays would soon be here, she decided she had no choice but to return. There was no one else who could possibly penetrate her dull mind with some measure of success, but Hughes. He believed he could teach her, and that was good enough for her. Now if she could only change her attitude regarding her own feelings of ineptitude and gain some confidence in herself, she just very well might learn to play—enough at least to entertain her father's guests.

Then she told herself, *Be honest, you want to see him again.*

That afternoon, she dressed carefully in a pink woolen day gown with a modest rounded neckline edged in cream-colored lace. When she arrived at Hughes' School of Music, she blushed when she saw the way Master Hughes stared at her, from the top of her upswept hair to the fine tan-colored boots on her feet. There was no question that, from the look in his eyes, he liked what he saw. Annabelle chose the pink gown, knowing that it brought out the best of her coloring and features.

Nodding his approval, he said, "You look fetching, Miss Watkins. Ready to tear down any barriers to playing Chopin today?"

With a groan she said, "For certain, I will give it my best effort."

In the music room, she sat down before the piano and prepared to play the dreaded Chopin once more.

Jasper spent the first hour instructing her, tapping out the notes against the top of the piano to help her find the rhythm as she played. Soon she was able to play the piece, start to finish, with only a few mistakes. She ended the piece confident that she had played it better than the last time, but she refused to look at her teacher.

She knew he'd sunk into the same chair he'd sat in two days earlier when Millie had played so dreadfully. Now, he sat in silence. After a while, when he didn't speak, she cautiously looked at him over her shoulder and found his blue-eyed gaze delving deep into hers.

"Well," he said as he slowly rose and ambled toward her. "That was…interesting."

Interesting? Not quite the flattering praise she'd expected to hear, but it was better than horrible, she supposed.

"It only took an hour and a half of my time to teach you the piece, and you played it fairly well."

Fairly well? True, she knew it hadn't been perfect still she thought her efforts deserved better than a fairly well. But then, this was the infamous musical genius who expected perfection from his students.

"Oh, I know once I practice it a few more times it'll be perfect."

"Yes, it will." He stopped beside her. "And I expect you to fulfill your promise to practice at least two hours a day."

"I will," Annabelle promised, knowing she would, feeling more confident now that she wouldn't disappoint her father.

"Let's move onto the next piece that your father wants you to learn then, shall we?"

The following week, Annabelle appeared for her two-hour lessons on the designated three days and made slow progress. The music grew more difficult, and though her practices helped, it just didn't seem to be enough to enable her to quickly learn all of the pieces perfectly. She found herself stumbling over several passages and her heart sank with dread, somehow guessing, from the silence in the music room, that he was growing more and more disappointed in her.

They worked closely together on the next piece of music, with him leaning over her shoulder often, guiding her fingers over the keys, hitting the right notes with her. He was a supreme teacher, and she was, for the most part, glad that she'd returned.

At the same time, her nerves were in shreds. Each time he leaned over her back and shoulders, cocooning her between his arms and body, shivers traveled up her spine. Each time he laid his hands gently upon her fingers, guiding her in the music, she found herself leaning back against him. The first time she'd done this, he had abruptly backed away from her, but not now. Now, he seemed to lean even closer. Shivers filtered up her spine when she felt his lips close to her ear, his gentle breathing against her neck.

Jasper couldn't keep his thoughts on anything but Annabelle.

He'd been proud of how she'd learned the first pieces of music, and of how she seemed to be making strides in this new one, but there was a problem; he couldn't keep his hands or thoughts off her. She struggled to learn the new piece and he knew that part of the reason was because of his self-imposed close proximity to her. Disgusted with his baser needs and feelings for this young woman, he tried to keep his hands away, to maintain some semblance of distance, but found it impossible.

He wanted Annabelle more than he'd ever wanted any other woman, addressing his innermost feelings for the first time in years. Being honest with himself, he realized that he'd been looking for her in every woman he met, every woman whom he'd courted, every woman who'd been his mistress. Perhaps he'd been in love with her all those years ago, even though she'd been of a tender age.

Now, faced with her presence again, he was uncertain what to do. At first, he believed his feelings were simply lust, but it was more than that. Dare he say it could be love? Never before had he felt more than just physical attraction for a woman.

She sat stiffly in front of him as she played the piece from the beginning once more. He paced away from her, listening, enjoying her playing. But as soon as he drew close, she proceeded to make errors. He smiled, knowing for certain now that she was as affected by his nearness, just as he was by hers.

"Stop a moment, Annabelle," he said softly, leaning over her once more.

Her lavender perfume drove him mad. The scent of her newly washed tresses drew his touch. Lifting his hand, he smoothed the hair at one temple, leaned down, and brushed his lips against that same spot. He heard her sigh, which encouraged him to wind his left arm around her waist, pulling her close against his chest.

"What are you doing?" she whispered, groaning when he gently bit her earlobe.

"Kissing you." *Though I desire much more.* "Tell me you object and I'll stop, but I know that I'll find it difficult, if not impossible, for you've captured my interest, sweet Miss Annabelle." *Possibly, my heart.*

Jasper noticed how she closed her eyes and her breathing grew ragged. "And you've captured mine, Master Hughes. But this is purely lust, isn't it?"

Was that disappointment he heard in her voice? "Call it what you like. All I know is that I want you more than I've wanted any other woman in a long, long time." Then, with a growl, he added, "Say my name, not my title."

"Jasper," she whispered in response to his command. "Move back, please."

He did so immediately, stunned by her spurning him when, just a moment ago, she seemed to welcome his advances. But then she spun around on the piano bench and launched herself into his embrace, a smile on her lips. "I want you, too, Jasper."

Joy tore through him and he laughed and lifted her into his arms. Then he carried her to the divan. There, he sank down to the cushions and for the first time kissed her lips. With her arms around his neck, she pressed her body fully against him. His heart stalled at the sweet contact.

She released his lips and spoke. "Jasper?"

He smiled down at her as he sat beside her on the divan. "What is it?"

"I want you. Make love to me."

His heart soared at the idea but then reason inserted itself into his mind. "Just kisses for now, do you understand? Though I'd like nothing better than to take you to my bed, we can't." he said, forthright.

"Yes, but—"

"No talking now, just feel."

At her nod, he breathed a relieved sigh.

With his lips pressed to hers, his kiss changed to one of rampant desire. After a long while, he broke away from her and met her wide-eyed, lust-filled gaze. Unable to hold back his desire, he dipped his head once more. Kissing a path down the soft creamy skin of her cheeks and neck, wanting more, much more, but he held himself back.

"Please, Jasper, more. I need more! Don't stop." She sat up and reached behind her.

"What is it you need, darling?" he whispered against her throat.

"Your lips on my…on my…oh! You know what I mean."

He chuckled. "I do indeed but we can't. Just kisses…only kisses," he murmured against her lips. He kissed her with more fervency but kept control of himself as he pressed her down to the divan once more.

Annabelle moaned and raised her hips from the divan. He felt his erection grow and thought what he wouldn't do for this woman. What he wouldn't give to have her beneath him, but he couldn't—wouldn't.

"I want you, Jasper," she begged. "Please, please…"

He sighed and moved back slightly. "No. We can't indulge ourselves more than a few kisses. You are a virgin and will one day be some man's wife. I will not ruin you for him. Do you understand me?"

She frowned as she wound her arms around his neck once more. "I don't care about that! I want you, so please continue."

He chuckled. "Oh, you would change your mind by morning, believe me."

He wouldn't offer for her; he couldn't. He'd vowed to live a solitary life—he enjoyed the quiet—enjoyed not having the responsibility of a wife and children. As he looked down upon her sweet, well-kissed lips, her eyes closed, looking ethereal and heartbreakingly lovely, he guessed that she would likely shake up his lonely existence. But he also knew he wouldn't be able to make the commitment to her she would want—would expect—a commitment she well deserved as a wife.

4

Annabelle was lost in a blissful euphoria, her entire focus on the feel of Jasper's lips on hers, his arms around her, holding her against his strong body.

"More, I need more," she groaned. "I love you!"

His kisses grew wild and savage. Her hips kept rising, seeking completion. When she started mewling and pulling at his hair for more, he abruptly released her and stood up from the divan, to her great disappointment.

"Oh, my!" Annabelle gasped as she sat up, breathing hard. Heat swarmed over her skin as she thought about the intimacy of his kisses, and that falling-off-the-cliff sensation left her wanting more —much more. Never had she experienced such cataclysmic sensations. She wanted him to do it again…but more than kisses.

Annabelle closed her eyes when he turned away from her. He went to stand in front of one long window, arm braced on the woodwork above it, staring out at the end of another day. She looked down and noticed her gown was a crumpled mess, and she smoothed it with her hands. His back was ramrod straight and he appeared cool, arrogant, as he had in the past.

What had she done by encouraging his kisses? And now, did he resent her for begging him for more? Oh, he must think her nothing but a hussy! Now what would happen? Would he continue teaching her, or would he not?

"Jasper?" she called softly as she walked toward him.

She came to a halt, and pain sliced through her at his next words. "Stop, Annabelle. I've made a terrible mistake."

Mistake? No! What we shared was wonderful.

Perhaps for him it had been a mistake; she had noticed he hadn't experienced the same intense feelings she had. Her cheeks flushed with humiliation.

He turned to face her, and she averted her eyes, unable to meet the look there—one of disgust, she guessed. She felt certain that she wasn't up to his standards regarding womanly attributes. Still, he wouldn't have kissed her as he had if he hadn't been attracted to her, would he?

She would be honest with him. Then she groaned inside as she suddenly recalled, in the heat of their passion, the words she'd said. "I love you." She'd said them, aloud, she realized, which told her why he was so aloof now. He didn't love her, and now she had to analyze her own feelings. Did she truly love him, or had she said them because she'd been in the throes of passion?

Had she meant the words, she mused, doubting her own feelings. She thought that she might love him in time, but not yet. Not now. *Liar!* the little voice inside her said. She would not have laid herself out on his divan like a woman of the night if she hadn't felt love for him.

Annabelle sniffed back her tears. Obviously, the man regretted what he'd done. And now it appeared he meant to run her off. No, she wouldn't leave—not just yet—not until she'd learned all of the music.

Striking a nonchalant pose, one hand on her hip, head tilted provocatively, she gave him a long, passionate look. "Well, then, good evening, Jasper. Perhaps next time, I may return the favor."

She turned on her heel and headed for the front door, believing her non-clingy attitude would calm him. Before she reached it, he'd grasped her wrist and pulled her around. Jasper wore a furious expression, yet his tone was cool.

"No games will you play with me, sweetheart. I have played every one of them, so I know what's what. I heard you say you love me."

She shrugged again and pulled her arm from his grasp. "If I did, I didn't mean the words. Call it impetuous words of the moment that are insignificant. Now I really must be going."

Annabelle turned to leave but he grasped her arm once more. "I don't want to lose you, but I cannot offer you marriage. I'm not the marrying kind."

His bluntness astonished her, but she kept her head about her and shrugged again. "I've a friend who tells me all men say that, but they eventually change their minds."

"Not me. Not ever, so do not pin your hopes on me as a husband." Pulling her close, he added, "But that doesn't mean we can't have something very special between us, does it?"

Narrowing her eyes on him, she snapped, "Such as?"

"I'm in dire need of a mistress."

She gasped.

He'd done the ultimate damage this time—he'd made her feel cheap. She pressed her palms against his chest until he released her, and reaching up, she slapped his right cheek. "Look elsewhere for a woman to fulfill your baser needs," she spat. Giving him a derisive look, she added, "I won't be requiring your services any longer, thank you very much."

Snatching up her skirts, she ran to the door, but she heard him coming up quickly behind her. She hadn't waited to stay for fear of viewing the horrible fury on his face, guilt setting in that she'd struck him. But he'd had no right to talk to her the way he had! She was surprised when he brought her to a halt and she found herself staring up into his remorseful expression.

Pulling her close, even though she fought against him, he wound his arms around her carefully and murmured against her hair, "Sorry, so sorry, Annabelle. I'm a beast of the worst kind. Please, accept my apology. I don't know what I was thinking to say such a thing to you."

She reached up and cupped his face with her hands, gazing into the remorseful expression in his eyes. "I wonder, too, what you were thinking. Your words were hurtful, Jasper. Is that truly how you think of me then? Being nothing more than your mistress?"

Jasper leaned his forehead against hers tenderly. "I admit the idea had crossed my mind. Forgive me."

"So, what you said then, about not being the marrying kind —'tis true?"

He sighed and released her. "Unfortunately, yes, and I have my reasons. Let us leave it at that for now. I'd truly like for you to finish your lessons with me. Will you return?"

Annabelle nodded. "If you believe you can still work with me."

"I can, but can you work with me?"

"Yes, I can put this all aside for the ultimate reward of learning the music."

"The last two pieces are very difficult. Are you up for the challenge?"

"I am, and I will learn to play them. Good night, Jasper."

She stood on tiptoe and pecked his cheek, a quick sisterly kiss good night, utterly ridiculous since all she wanted was for him to make love to her. Choking back her laughter at the surprised expression on Jasper's face, she turned and fled.

Jasper stood in the open doorway, saw a footman help her into her carriage, and watched as she rode away.

Shutting the door, he leaned back against it and closed his eyes with a groan. How in the hell would he be able to keep things platonic between them for the next lessons when all he wanted to do was tear her clothes away from her body and enter her sweet, honeyed core? Lord, but if he weren't a confirmed bachelor, if he hadn't seen and experienced firsthand his parents' volatile relationship which had led them to divorce, he'd marry Annabelle.

Was that one reason—his parents' botched marriage—enough anymore to remain a bachelor? He didn't think so, not anymore. After Annabelle's music event, he'd deal with his feelings for her, but not now. She needed to learn the music well enough to play for the event, and he would pound the music into her if necessary.

Two days later, Annabelle sat at the piano in Jasper's studio, playing the same bars, over and over. This new piece was much more difficult than the first three pieces she'd learned. She began again, for the tenth time, her confidence of the previous days' accomplishments dwindling. She could tell by Jasper's curtness that he was growing impatient.

"Stop! Enough!" Jasper finally shouted.

Annabelle had never been a gifted sight-reader. It took her an awful long time to match up the music notes on the pages to her fingers. She was slow, pathetically slow in learning this new piece, unable to advance with any competence through the first four bars of music after nearly an hour of work.

"Perhaps if we move on to one of my father's other requests?" she suggested.

Jasper shook his head and paced the length of the music room. Every now and then, he would toss his long hair, then it would fall back down to his tense shoulders.

Annabelle was enthralled by his movements, his form tall and lean, lips firm and full. She recalled how his lips had felt on hers and she sighed, her cheeks heating up at the thought of that one evening. Would an older, worldly man like him ever think about her romantically? Lust—she knew he'd felt that for her for certain, and he hadn't minced words about his feelings on the matter, including his awful invitation to be his mistress.

Finally, he paused in his pacing and stared at her from across the room. "It won't help to move on to any other pieces, as you are not following my instructions with this piece. How many times must I tell you to straighten your spine and not bend yourself over the keys? How many times must I remind you to uncurl your fingers on the keys? How many times must I remind you to follow the rhythm with my taps? You aren't listening to me. We'll stop for the day as I don't think you're capable of doing much more, unfortunately."

Annabelle felt deflated, defeated. She also felt his expectations for her learning were exceedingly far-fetched. She was no musical genius and he knew it, although up until now he had been patient.

Annabelle defended herself. "I've only been at this an hour."

"Ten days until Christmas. That is all the time you have to learn the songs. Or, are you satisfied with playing just the three you've learned?"

"Oh, no, three is not enough! Perhaps if you gave me a lesson every day…" She bit her lip and added, "Wait, I've an idea. I'll play the three you've taught me, then you could perform the rest!"

He looked down his nose at her. "I do not play for the public, as I'm sure you are aware."

Annabelle knew he had gone into retirement at a relatively young age and wondered why. From what she'd seen from him over the last few weeks, he seemed to play magnificently and told him so. "Why! You are flawless in your playing, Jasper. I can't see any reason why you can't perform at my father's event."

He shook his head. "No, and that's final. Besides, this would be an easy way out of this situation for you, wouldn't it? As far as lessons with me every day, it's not possible. I've several other students on those alternate days when you do not come. No, I must find another method to instruct you."

"What other method?"

"I'll have to think about it. I've a cancellation tomorrow and am available between three and five in the afternoon. Come then and I'll have arrived at another way to teach you that will hopefully prove to be more successful."

❁

At his dinner table that evening, Jasper racked his brain as he tried to think of another method to teach Annabelle. Suddenly, memories of his second music instructor entered his mind.

Master Harrison McMahon had hailed from Scotland and had been a cold, strict teacher. Jasper had been ten years old at the time and on the cusp of being considered a genius. Master McMahon was convinced that Jasper's total dedication—practicing each day for long hours— would turn him into the prodigy that he believed he was. The man had been right.

After two years of instruction with Master McMahon, several moments spent draped over the piano bench with his drawers down, as the master beat his bottom raw with a wicked, whippy cane, Jasper had learned at a quicker pace. Master McMahon was satisfied that his student did indeed become the premier musical prodigy he believed him to be.

Would a bit of corporal punishment help Annabelle learn the music?

No, he couldn't do it. She was no ten-year-old child, but a gentlewoman, full grown. He smiled then at the thought of her draped across his piano bench, her dress tossed up, revealing the curves of her sweet bottom. He couldn't do it, he couldn't! She'd hate him, she'd protest, she could possibly never want to see him again.

He would have to think of something else.

※

The next day, Annabelle arrived late at Jasper's studio, at half-past three, amidst a raging snowstorm. Her carriage had become stuck twice in the snow, hence the reason for her late arrival. When her driver insisted they turn back, she'd refused, telling him she couldn't miss her lesson.

Jasper had been worried sick about her when she hadn't arrived at her lesson time, praying she had turned back home. Therefore, he was surprised, pleased, yet irritated to see her standing, covered with snow, on his doorstep. He pulled her inside then rushed past her and down the stairs to her carriage.

He gave her driver money. "Stay at the Fox Tavern tonight. And pay for accommodations for Miss Watkins as well. I'll see that she gets there safe and sound after her lesson."

"Aye, thank you, sir," the young man said before whipping the horses into a trudging gait down the street, slowly maneuvering through the building snow.

Inside, Annabelle sat before the fire in his parlor, warming her hands. Stopping in the doorway, he cleared his throat. She looked up at him and smiled. He smiled in return but said as he came to her side, "Did you truly believe one more day's lesson would help you learn the pieces?"

"You know I can't afford to miss a single minute, Jasper. I have to try."

He nodded. "Yes, you are right, though this snow should have been a deterrent. Come then, we won't waste any more time."

While he'd much rather show her pieces of heaven again in his arms, he knew they had to tend to the task at hand. After the holidays, he would approach her and her father about marriage, having put his feelings aside regarding his parents' failed marriage.

He'd come to the decision that he was besotted with Annabelle and refused to let her go. She was no young girl, but at the age of twenty-two a bit long in the tooth as far as finding a suitable husband, though he admitted he knew of several older widowed men at his club who eagerly took to wife spinster women and widows. Was that the way of it then? Once a man tasted marriage, he couldn't live without it? Perhaps. All he knew was Annabelle Watkins was perfect for him, and he would not lose her to another.

He smiled when she sat eagerly before the piano and started playing the new piece. He paced back and forth as he listened to the first bars, cringing when she started striking the wrong notes in the same places that she had done before.

"You haven't practiced, have you?" he asked, tapping her on one shoulder. She stopped playing and bit her lower lip, not meeting his eyes.

"No, I didn't get a chance, I'm afraid," she murmured.

"I won't ask why and can only assume you had other pressing things to do." He made his voice icy, remote. She just hung her head and wouldn't look at him. He heaved a deep sigh. "Try it again."

She did, and it was no better the second time. "Again," he snapped.

Annabelle resumed but made the same mistakes. Jasper saw the more he insisted she try the worse mistakes she made. Yet she didn't appear nervous, so he moved to his desk and picked up a music baton, coming to a decision.

When she started again, he stood at her side, raised the baton, and tapped the notes on the piano's top in an effort to keep her on time. Her timing didn't improve, nor did her playing. Irritation flooded him. The fact she hadn't practiced angered him. And if word got out about this it could harm his reputation.

With controlled deliberation, he lifted the stick and tapped her once briskly across the knuckles of the hand nearest him.

Annabelle gasped, pulled her hands off the keys, and she stared at him in disbelief, her eyes wide.

Perhaps now she'd understand when he said he expected her to practice that she would. She started rising to her feet when he said, "Keep your seat, Miss Watkins. We are not through with this lesson."

5

"You struck me!" she shouted, her voice quivering as she sank down on the bench.

"You deserved it for you've made the same mistakes over and over again. Now, try once more, please."

She stared at him, her eyes untrusting, her lips trembling. Yet, he hardened his heart, telling himself that she would learn the music, even if it meant turning her over his knee. She had come to him for instruction and he'd tried his best with his usual methods, and they hadn't worked.

Then, a tiny voice inside him said that perhaps this is as far as she can go, as far as she can learn.

No, he refused to believe it, for while he believed she was no prodigy, she was an intelligent woman who had the ability to learn to play, if she spent the time practicing the pieces.

She glared at him a moment but then resumed playing.

He ambled around the piano, listening, nodding. When she finished the bars perfectly—a piece she'd been trying to play for two days, he said, "Better." With a cool look, he met her teary eyes.

"See what a bit of encouragement can do? Let us move onto the next bars."

She gazed at him and he caught the sad, untrusting look in her eyes. Harden your heart, man. Think of your reputation…

Damn! That wasn't the reason the cool voice inside him said; she'd provided an undeniable challenge to him and hadn't she told him she wanted her playing to be perfect for her father's party? She would succeed, if she applied herself.

When she started with the new bars, they proved to be as torturous as the first ones had. He swore under his breath, reached out with the baton, and rapped her knuckles again.

"Ow!" She pulled her hands from the keys, her eyes spitting fire. She grabbed the baton from him before he realized what she was about to do, and then broke it in half over her knee, tossing the pieces to the floor. Why he was stunned he had no idea, since he'd seen her fury unleashed upon him seven years ago. He had to admit a roar of passion soared through him at her fury.

"How dare you!" she shouted, at the same time rising to her feet and tipping the bench over in her haste.

Annabelle Watkins' fury had angered him yet thrilled him at the same time years ago. She was magnificent, with her tresses loosed from her pins, tumbling down to her shoulders, her cheeks colored crimson, and her eyes sparkling in rage. He nearly laughed aloud at her anger but then thought better of it. Who was the teacher here and who the student?

He bent over, righted the bench, and put on his most severe face. "Sit down on that bench, Miss Watkins. You have much to learn."

"As do you," she snarled. "How dare you strike me? How could you, and after what…after what we shared…"

All he thought about in that moment was himself. Perhaps, if he'd still been able to perform, he wouldn't worry so much about his reputation as a premier instructor being ruined. He frowned then, thinking of how she had uttered those three little words to him, and he said, "We shared passion, nothing more than that. Do you understand? Now, I won't allow you to ruin my reputation, so you will learn these songs." Damn! He knew this was no way to talk to her—the woman he believed he loved and wanted to marry. But his anger got the better of him.

Her lower lip trembled. She didn't speak nor would she meet his eyes. Turning from him, she took a couple of strides, but he stopped her, reaching out and grasping her forearm.

"You're not leaving yet."

"I'm through for the day."

"You are through when I decide, Miss Watkins."

❦

Annabelle couldn't believe the man's audacity. Whatever made her believe she loved him? He was a tyrannical, self-centered man with only a worry for himself and his reputation as a music instructor. She knew it would be a waste of time telling him that no one would care if he failed in teaching her how to play the piano—no one.

Gritting her teeth, she said, "I said, I am through."

He moved to the doorway, blocking her exit. "You require a lesson in obedience. Mayhap it will help you in learning to play the piano. Discipline, that's what you need, Miss Watkins."

"Perhaps I do," she said, "but not your method." She paused directly in front of him. "I won't ask you again to move, sir."

"Good, because I'm not planning on it." He pointed toward the piano. "I said, back to the bench."

Annabelle planted both hands against his chest and shoved. Much to her disappointment, he didn't budge. She tried again, but he remained rock solid in position, blocking her exit. Then he grinned, and her world turned red. Without thinking, she lifted her foot and pulled it back, ready to kick him in the shins.

She caught the warning look in his eyes, and in his voice when he said, "You kick me and you will be very, very sorry."

She let fly her kid leather boot, ignoring his threat. After delivering one swift kick, Annabelle paused in her flight to watch him lift his leg, grab his shin, and hop around the floor, swearing under his breath as he left the exit open for her.

Satisfied that he wouldn't be coming after her, she turned the knob and opened the door. "Good evening to you, Jasper. I won't require any more lessons. Father will just have to be happy with the three songs I've learned. Besides, most of those bluebloods will likely not even realize I'm playing the same songs over and over again."

In the hallway, she snatched her coat off a hook, conscious of the fact that he was coming after her. She heard his strides behind her—limping strides she thought, covering her mouth with her hand to stifle her laughter. Lord, but what the man caused her to do! Never had she struck anyone—man or woman—but strike him she had, and with little thought and no feelings of repentance. He'd deserved the kick, and so much more in her opinion.

"I won't allow you to walk out that door on me again, Annabelle!" he shouted.

Again? Oh, he must be thinking of the first time. Annabelle looked at him over her shoulder, to where he stood leaning against a wall, seemingly still favoring his leg.

She opened the door. "Watch me."

Annabelle ran down the snow-covered steps, hanging onto the banister. On the sidewalk, she rushed to the location where her coach always awaited her but found the spot vacant. Looking around, her eyes widened in horror when she saw no one on the streets. The snow had fallen heavily, and it continued to fall. She could barely see a foot in front of her through the flurries. Lifting her skirts, she trudged through the snow, arriving at the corner, and peering around it. No coach.

Digging in her pocket, she found a handkerchief and dabbed at her eyes, realizing that she dabbed at tears, not snow. She started walking again. The streets were quiet and eerie, so she was grateful that the city streetlamps lightened her way. Suddenly, a lone coach appeared. She waved her hand and called out, "Here!"

The coach stopped in front of her. Disappointment set in when she saw it wasn't her coach. The door opened, and two men hopped down. They were big and brutish, and a bad feeling came over her when she saw their lewd expressions. Annabelle started backing away.

"Lookie here, Johnny. Look what the good Lord left for us. Our very own doxie." The younger man reached out to grasp her arm. She jumped back, hiked up her skirts, and took two running steps. A hand landed on her shoulder, pulling her up short and spun her around.

The man grinned evilly, and she caught the glint of gold in his mouth. He wound a hard arm around her waist and hauled her up and off her feet. Bracing herself in the opening of the coach, she screamed, "Jasper! Help!"

❦

Jasper stood on his stoop as he watched Annabelle trudge through the snow. She stopped at the corner, looked up and down the street. Jasper groaned, recalling how he'd told her coachman to take a room for the night and to hold one for Annabelle, guessing travel would be impossible.

He slammed the door, retrieved his long woolen coat from a closet. He also pulled a gun down from the closet shelf, thinking with this late hour he couldn't be too careful, even though his residence was located in one of the best neighborhoods in the city.

Then, he found his walking stick behind the door, thinking another weapon might be advisable as well. He shoved the gun into his deep coat pocket, strode out the door and into the cold night. The inn was located a block down and around the corner. Annabelle may think him a cad, but he wasn't. A cad would have left her out in the snow to her own devices instead of walking her to the inn, as he planned. As he rushed through the snow, guilt plagued him. He shouldn't have struck her with that damned baton. What he should have done was hauled her over his knee and laid into her with a hard hand. He sighed, somehow knowing that treatment wouldn't work with Miss Annabelle, either.

As he headed down the sidewalk, he saw Annabelle raising her hand to stop a passing coach. Saw the driver and then a man exit the coach and confront her. Then one of them made the mistake of putting a hand on her.

Anger flared inside Jasper. Tucking his cane under his arm, he ran until he caught up to the coach, grinning when he heard Annabelle inside, screaming, "Let me out! I shall report you to the authorities if you don't."

Jasper yanked the door open. Leave it to his hot-headed student to cause a ruckus. He liked how she stood up for herself, even with him, he admitted. She was sitting across from the big ruffian, feet kicking, hands striking out. The man held his hands out to protect himself, but Annabelle was a whirling dervish of energy and anger.

Reaching inside, Jasper hauled the man out of the coach. The ruffian pulled his arm back, fist ready to strike Jasper—until he saw the gun Jasper aimed between his eyes. "Leave," Jasper warned, "before I change my mind and put you out of your miserable life."

The man ran away down the snow-covered street. The coach

driver leaped to the ground from the opposite side and ran off, following his companion. Turning his gaze on Annabelle, Jasper found her sitting in the coach, her arms wrapped around her body. He reached inside and hauled her out and into his arms.

Jasper realized then that only her anger had fired her fury to resist the men. He thanked heaven for her strength and courage in that moment. Now she trembled and rubbed her face against his wool coat. He heard her shuddering and knew that she was crying, even though she tried to conceal the fact.

"Crying won't offend me," he murmured against her hair, tightening his arms around her.

She sniffled then chuckled as she arched back and looked up at him. "No, but it will offend me. Oh, did you see the look on that man's face when he saw your gun? It was priceless."

He grinned and, reaching up, he pushed one tendril of hair off her forehead and behind her ear. "It was, wasn't it?" His grin diminished. "Never run off on me like that again. You could be dead now if I hadn't followed you."

She pulled herself completely out of his arms and crossed them over her breasts. Her eyes glinted up at him and she gave him a pouting look.

"No pouting," he ordered. "Good God, woman, you suddenly look like the girl I knew seven years ago."

"I am still that girl, and you are still that same infuriating teacher. God, I hated how you had no humor, though I admit you've improved somewhat. You appear a bit less intense."

"You shouldn't have run away."

She sighed. "I know, but you shouldn't have struck me. Even when my father spanked me when I was small, it didn't improve my behavior."

"Yes, I see what you mean," he said dryly. "I've learned my lesson well."

"The three songs I've learned will be enough. I thank you for coming to my aid this night, Jasper, but I really must get home or Father will worry."

"The snow's too deep. I found you lodgings at an inn. It's only a few blocks away, so I'll walk you there, and I'll send someone to inform your father."

At the Rose Inn, Jasper made sure she got to her room, and then he left her with the admonishment that he would see her on the morrow for another lesson.

"Tomorrow, ten a.m. sharp, I'll arrive and escort you to my home. We'll work through the day on learning the next piece."

"I don't think so, Jasper."

He frowned. "Don't be obstinate. The holidays are nearly upon us then what will you do?"

"As I said earlier, I'll play the three songs for Father's guests and be done with it."

Jasper's heart clenched when she stood in the open doorway to her room, reached up, and stroked his face. Raising herself up on her toes, she kissed him. He groaned and started to take her into his arms when she stepped back. "Good night, Jasper."

She closed the door on him. He was too stunned to protest or try to stop her. He called softly through the door. "If you don't show tomorrow, I'll be forced to come to your home."

"Please do. Father would enjoy seeing you again." He guessed then she would not be returning. He returned home and decided he'd wait a few days before making the decision to visit her at home. Then he fought with himself over the next several days, each day expecting Annabelle to arrive on his doorstep, but she didn't. He'd fought to stay away from her, his pride injured. Rejection was something he did not take well, hurt by her not returning for lessons.

His parents had been involved in society doings and had had

little time for him. He'd grown up with few friends since his entire life had been practice, practice, and more of it between performances, yet he'd never harbored any ill feelings toward those people in his past, nor had he given them more than a passing thought. He felt differently about Annabelle because he loved her.

He settled into his usual routine of his students arriving for their lessons, day after day, but there was no Annabelle. A few days before Christmas, which he would be spending alone as usual, he received an invitation to Annabelle's home for an evening of entertainment on Christmas Eve, dining, and dancing—a holiday celebration. Jasper knew that this was Annabelle's doing. Dig the knife in a bit deeper, my dear, he raged in silence. Did she want him to witness her playing, mistakes and all, knowing it would be humiliating for both of them? He didn't think Annabelle could ever be so vindictive. Apparently, he'd thought wrong. He returned the invitation with regrets.

Soon Christmas Eve arrived, and Jasper had made the decision to attend Annabelle's event after all, damning himself for not being strong enough to stay away. Plain and simple, after a little soul-searching, he couldn't stay away from the woman he loved. He would marry her...he must marry her...or go crazy. No other woman would do. He'd convinced himself that their marriage would be nothing like his parents'.

Arriving at her home, dressed in formal black attire that he hadn't worn in ages, he stood outside on her stoop, listening with his ear at the door. He'd arrived late, assuming all of the other guests would have arrived by now. He heard conversation, people laughing, and a violinist playing softly in the background. Finally, he raised his hand and knocked.

Immediately, the door opened and Harold, the long-standing Watkins butler, stood formally before him. He bowed. "Good evening, Master Hughes."

"Good evening to you, Harold. Good seeing you."

Harold nodded, his posture erect as usual, expression passive, although Jasper thought he saw a twinkling in the elderly man's eyes.

Jasper stepped inside, brushed the light flakes of snow from his coat, and then removed the garment and handed it to Harold. Jasper took a few steps toward the parlor, but he paused when Harold spoke urgently.

"Master Hughes, wait. I must announce you first."

Waving a negligent hand, Jasper replied, "No need. I want to surprise Miss Annabelle."

"Ah, well then," Harold said, "You're just in time to hear her play."

Lucky me, Jasper thought dryly as he moved with long strides toward the parlor. He paused in the doorway, the double-wide doors thrown open to make use of all the space in the large parlor room. Chairs had been set up similar to a theater's seating, rows of ten seats with an aisle separating them, five on each side. Upon a quick perusal, Jasper decided forty people were in attendance—some of them he recognized as icons of New York society.

Scanning the room, he saw Annabelle's father move from his position near the fireplace and come to him with a broad smile on his lips.

Arthur Watkins shook hands with Jasper. "How can I thank you for taking time from your busy schedule to teach my Annabelle? Why, she's improved tremendously just from those few lessons," he boasted.

"You've heard her then?" Jasper asked hesitantly.

Arthur nodded. "She's been practicing for days, and she plays beautifully, thanks to you. So glad you could attend this evening. Come, I've saved you a seat close to the piano."

"That wouldn't be a good idea, sir," Jasper said. "My close

proximity will make Annabelle nervous. I'll take a seat here in the back, if you don't mind."

Arthur frowned. "Well, of course, if that is what you want." He turned and looked toward the piano when he heard music. "It seems my daughter is ready to begin. "I shall see you after Annabelle's performance."

"Of course." Heaving a deep sigh, Jasper took a glass of wine from a waiter before tossing back the tails of his dove-tailed jacket and sinking onto a chair. Luckily, no one else sat beside him, for he didn't want to face anyone's censure once they heard Annabelle play. Afterward, he vowed, he'd make a quick exit, before anyone could ask questions.

Jasper heard Arthur say, "May I present, for your listening pleasure this evening, my daughter, Annabelle."

He had to crane his neck and half-rise from his seat to see her, and his heart pounded loudly in his chest when he saw her wheat-colored tresses arranged in a braided coronet on her head. She wore a sapphire-colored gown that enhanced the blueness of her eyes and the creamy colored complexion of her skin. She curtsied prettily then sat on the piano bench, ready to play.

Sinking low in his seat, Jasper decided if she couldn't see him, she'd play without any errors, damning himself for ever having struck her during the last lesson. Pride—his damned pride—he'd believed had been at stake, just as it would be now. But now he realized he didn't care; if he had he wouldn't have showed up to hear Annabelle play.

Joining in with the mild yet friendly and controlled applause, Jasper afterward sank back in his seat, ready to hear her begin. Immediately, she launched into the first Chopin piece he'd taught her. His heart nearly came to an abrupt halt when she started, readying himself for her mistakes, but he relaxed when she played the entire song with no breaks, no mistakes, and with heartfelt delight. Satisfaction settled deep inside him at the thought she'd improved greatly in the last week since he'd seen her.

At the last few dwindling notes, all was quiet. The guests then exploded into riotous applause, and "Brava! Brava!" could be heard throughout the parlor. She took her bow and Jasper wanted to rise, move to her side, and take her in his arms, but knew he couldn't. She launched into the second and third pieces, and she played each one perfectly, with spirit and with heart—so much heart that Jasper felt tears welling in his eyes.

But that was all that she knew, he recalled, riveted in place, ready to hear her begin again with the first piece, but she surprised him. She launched into a popular holiday carol, then another, and another, each followed by appreciative applause. She ended her performance with "Silent Night," and Jasper saw more than one tearful-eyed guest in the audience. By the time she ended the song, Jasper had learned one important thing—it did not matter that she couldn't play all of the challenging songs of the virtuoso pianists. What mattered was that she played what she knew well. She would never be talented as her mother, but that didn't matter to Jasper. Her talent was unique, her own, and she was lovely.

He came to his feet and applauded with the other guests, throwing in his own "Brava!" The guests quieted when Annabelle spoke then. He stayed in his seat, slumping low to avoid her finding him, wondering what she would say. Probably flail him with her tongue for his awful attempts at teaching her, he decided, and he'd deserve that flailing.

"Well, it seems my illustrious teacher has left already for the night," she murmured.

Groaning inside, he mused, so she had been searching for him. Damn her father for telling her he'd shown up.

The guests turned, moved their bodies to the sides to make a path down the center of the chairs, revealing Jasper's presence.

Annabelle's smile called to him as she held out her hand. "Master Jasper Hughes, ladies and gentlemen. The best teacher a student could ever have. Come up here. No need to be shy," she said. Grinning, her white teeth shining, dimples showing, she stood there, gazing only at him as she held out her tiny hand, inviting him to share her stage.

Oh, she would pay for this, he mused, as he rose to his full height, bowing in appreciation to the generous applause. Tears filled his eyes once more, and he gulped down the growing lump in his throat as he made his way up the aisle, stopping beside her. He took her hand, kissed it, and pulled her close to his side. With his eyes only on her, he leaned over her and said, "You shouldn't be sharing your spotlight with me, Annabelle."

"I choose to," she said, adding softly, "I choose you. Whether as your sweetheart, mistress, or wife, I choose you, and you can't get rid of me."

He narrowed his eyes and whispered, "Are you threatening me?"

Reaching up, she placed her hands on either side of his face, then kissed his lips. Gasps and murmurs from the guests erupted, followed by profound silence.

It took all of Jasper's power not to scoop her up in his arms and leave the holiday party behind. He wanted to be alone with her and not share her with anyone. When she ended the kiss, she whispered, "Absolutely. So what will you do about it?"

6

Heaving a dramatic sigh, aware of the silence in the parlor, he sank to one knee, kissed her hand once more, and said, "Marry me, Miss Annabelle. Make me the happiest of all men. Be my wife."

Gasps of surprise and pleasure, whispers, and gossip swirled through the parlor, but then the room quieted again, seemingly waiting for her response.

Jasper caught the tears in her eyes, and when they started falling and sliding down her cheeks, he nearly rose to crush her in his arms and reassure her that he loved her. He couldn't say it in public, he couldn't, but she knew he loved her—she must—for he went down on his knee for her.

"Yes," she choked out, "and you will make me the happiest of all women, this Christmas, and forever more Christmases."

He rose amid the applause and shrieks of delight exploding from the guests as he took her into his arms, pulling her against his body and lifting her from her feet. He kissed her for the longest time, ending it when he knew he must. Setting her on her feet, he caught the dazed, surprised look of love on her face. Then, as he looked beyond her, he caught her father's pleased expression. Jasper reluctantly released Annabelle when her father strode up and took his daughter into his arms. "I am happy with your choice, Annabelle."

"I am glad for if you were not, I am afraid I would be compelled to disobey you and do as I please."

Arthur released Annabelle then held out his hand to Jasper. "I cannot think of a finer man for a husband than you, Hughes."

Suddenly, the guests swarmed them with congratulations, and toasts made to the newly engaged couple. Then, several people crowded around them, begging Jasper to play.

It had been five years since Jasper had played for a crowd, and now he was uncertain. His one hand plagued him constantly with pain, brought about by muscle spasms that caused contortions. He wasn't ready to let the world know about his disability. Still, he didn't want to disappoint people, and he turned to Annabelle and said, "Play with me. Please?"

She nodded as they sank side by side onto the piano bench, close together, their thighs brushing, and laughing as they tried to find comfortable positions so they each could play. Jasper whispered, "You choose the first song."

"'Deck The Halls' then," Annabelle said decisively.

They launched into the tune and the guests crowded around them at the piano and sang along.

Jasper had lost his battle for freedom. No longer would he be a happy bachelor, but instead a deliriously satisfied, jubilant husband.

Later that evening, after the guests had left, and after Annabelle's father had gone to bed, Jasper sat with Annabelle on his lap on the divan before the fire, brushing the braids from her long fair tresses, breathing in her lavender scent. Chagrinned, he felt his body responding to her, and he adjusted her on his lap, changed his mind. and placed her on the divan between his legs.

She purred as he stroked the brush through her hair. Finally, he put it down on the table beside him, wrapped his arms around her waist, and held her tightly against his chest. Placing his chin on her shoulder, he stared into the fire, enjoying the feel of her in his arms and knowing that he would enjoy the sensation for a lifetime.

Annabelle turned her head toward him and he took her lips in a heated kiss, leaving her panting for air and her eyes glittering with desire. For him. She had been frankly surprised when her father had left her alone with Jasper, not insisting that he leave and that she retire for the night. But then, she supposed since they were engaged, it did not matter to him, which was a good thing since it seemed that neither Jasper nor she could keep their hands to themselves.

"We need to marry soon, Jasper," she whispered, "for I'm very much afraid you'll make me a fallen woman."

He chuckled and kissed her full on the lips again, squeezing each of her breasts in the palms of his hands. When he released her lips, he murmured, "Yes, but you'll be *my* fallen woman. And that's all that matters,"

"Fallen woman?" she said. "For some peculiar reason, I love the sound of that. When shall we begin? I don't believe I can wait until we're married."

He gave her a shocked look. "Why, Miss Annabelle Watkins, shame on you for your wantonness."

"But only with you, Jasper. Only with you."

"Well, then, that's different, isn't it? Hmm, perhaps you should come to my house on the morrow for a lesson."

"Why, what a splendid idea. But do you really think you can teach me more than you already have?"

"We will see what your capacity for learning is tomorrow. Come for the day. I have much to teach you."

"And I have much to learn as your willing student, Master Jasper Hughes."

Slowly lowering his lips to hers, he kissed her, thanking the heavens that they weren't talking about her learning to play the piano.

THE END

AUTHOR NOTE

Though a diagnosis hadn't been found yet for a debilitating illness called Focal Dystonia in 1890, Jasper Hughes possibly suffered from it.

Focal Dystonia is a neurological condition affecting a muscle or muscles in a part of the body, causing an undesirable muscular contraction or twisting, and sometimes pain. Several renowned musicians have been struck with the illness, to which there is no cure.

NIGHT MAGIC

In Depression-era Minnesota, Eleanor Swenson inherits her deceased parents' dream resort—six cabins in need of repair near the Canadian border. Lumberjack Riley Flaherty has recently lost his job. When Eleanor offers him a job as her "handyman" he gladly accepts, smitten by her beauty. When wild animals in the northern Minnesota woods threaten them into leaving, they don't give in, but discover true love beneath the northern lights.

Author Note:
Night Magic is also available in the anthology,
Romance and Mystery Under the Northern Lights.

September 1934

John Swenson slouched in his chair at O'Reilly's pub, drinking a tall mug of beer, his second of the evening. His flinty-eyed gaze swept around the pub, stopping now and again on one pretty woman then another.

"Stop staring at the ladies, John!" Eleanor Swenson scolded. "You're supposed to be finding a man for me."

John's laughter lifted above the raucous piano music across the room. "There's no reason why we can't kill two birds with one stone, is there, sis?" he asked, one eyebrow lifted.

Eleanor tossed a hank of unfashionable straight blonde hair over her back as she sat across from her brother. "I wouldn't need to be finding myself a man if you'd return home with me and help out at the resort."

He gave her a long, withering look. "That resort is not my home." Changing the topic, he tilted his head to one side and stared at her. "You know, you should do something about your hair."

"What's wrong with my hair?" she blustered.

"It's long, boring, and not quite the thing these days. You'd have a better chance of attracting a man if you cut and permed it."

"I refuse to waste a single cent on myself. You know how important the resort is to me. It's my livelihood, and I mean to make something of it."

"Sorry, sis. With this Depression, the place is losing money. People can't afford a vacation nowadays with so many out of work. Besides, why did our parents have to buy all of that land up north, nearly to the Canadian border anyway, for God's sake? I refuse to live away from civilization, and that's that. Now stop your fussing. I'll find you a nice sturdy man, one unafraid of physical labor. It just might take me some time is all," he murmured, his eyes on the waitress headed straight for their table.

"Another brew for you, sir?" she softly inquired.

With a small smile, John asked, "What's your name, darling?"

"Why…why, it's Maggie."

Eleanor took pity on the poor girl whose cheeks were turning pink as she grasped an empty beer mug in each hand. "We were just leaving, Maggie, so nothing more. Thank you."

"Oh, but don't leave on my account!" the waitress protested.

"I'm not," John said, his grin widening. "I'll have another brew. After the long dry spell we've had in this country, I have some catching up to do."

Eleanor rose from her seat. "I'll be at your house. I'm returning home in the morning."

"You just got here," he protested. "What's the rush?"

"A few fishermen are coming up from Iowa and I have a cabin to clean, that's what."

"Thought you said it's been a slow season."

"For summer it was. But this early fall, I've had a few come in, like this one tomorrow."

"I'm frankly amazed, but what the heck. Make hay while you

can, especially since winter will be here soon." He frowned. "Then what will you do?"

"I'll just hole up in my cabin for the entire season, same as last year."

"Fighting off bears again?"

"I hope not," she said, her voice trembling as she recalled several close encounters she'd had with roaming black bears on the resort property.

"Come home for the winter since you've no customers."

"I need to work to make the cabins more habitable, and winter is the season to do it," she said. "Remember? That's why I came down—to find someone to help me."

As she left the pub, she thought about her home, Swenson's Haven Resort, in northeastern Minnesota. Beauty and isolation surrounded her at the small resort.

Her parents had purchased several acres of lakeshore property on a large Canadian border lake called Crane ten years ago. They'd started the small vacation spot in 1928, before the stock market crashed. They built three small cabins and the following year, two more. Before rough times, the cabins had always been booked with guests, from mid-May until late October; guests wanting to experience the great outdoors, including fishing, hunting, and enjoying nature at its finest.

During late fall, an array of colors called the aurora borealis would paint the sky—a breathtaking sight unlike anything Eleanor had ever seen in her life. She couldn't wait to see it again.

Unfortunately, the cabins had never been insulated properly and were never meant for winter habitation, but Eleanor had chosen to live there year round. Insulating her cabin was necessary and she had no idea how to go about it. She'd tried using various items over the past winter, but nothing seemed to work well.

For Eleanor, born and raised in St. Paul—civilization, in

comparison—it hadn't been easy taking on the job of resort owner after her parents died in a boating accident the previous summer. She'd felt duty-bound to quit high school in her last year to carry on her parents' dream of building a flourishing resort. John, six years older, had helped her over that first summer, driving up each weekend. But when winter struck, he'd returned to St. Paul. He'd finished college with a degree in accounting and was one of the lucky few to have found a job in his field during these depressed economic times. Running a resort was the furthest thing from his mind.

She'd moved from the family home in St. Paul, where her brother still lived, to the main cabin at the resort. She shuddered when she thought about the bears, and other critters, roaming the wilderness around her cabin. When evening arrived, she'd been afraid to go outside, the various animal sounds and noises unnerving. She made sure to complete her nightly relieving in the outdoor bathroom before dark but kept a chamber pot under the bed for night emergencies. She'd viewed the northern lights from her cabin window, wishing it were safe to go outside.

Eleanor was convinced she'd learn over time to cohabitate with nature. She just needed a handyman who knew how to swing a hammer and pound a nail with accuracy. Knowing something about an electrician's work would be a help as well. She had big plans for her resort, including building bathrooms inside each cabin, plenty of insulation installed in all of the cabins, and a new furnace so she could live in hers comfortably all year.

She strode down the street, deep in thought, not noticing the appreciative glances from the men passing by. She wore a bias-cut dress with a cowl-neck that ended mid-calf, made of dark blue rayon. She was completely unaware of the pretty picture she made in the blue dress with her long blonde hair flowing down her back, a small matching blue hat perched on her head.

Pain struck her wrist then and she gasped when she glanced down and saw a hand snatch her handbag. She looked up in time to see an adolescent boy with a harried look on his face. Eleanor heard him mutter, "Sorry, ma'am," before he slammed his hands against her shoulders and shoved.

Twisting sideways as she fell, she landed on her side, grimacing when the outside of her leg scraped on the sidewalk. She rolled to a sitting position, but dizziness overcame her, and she lay down on her back, stunned, her eyes closed against the brilliant sunlight.

Then strong hands pulled her up and held her steady. Surrounded by a big man's body, her cheek pressed against scratchy wool, she shuddered against him.

"You all right, ma'am?"

Eleanor tried pulling away, but he cupped the back of her head and held her pressed against him. "I can't breathe," she managed, her hands pressing against his chest.

He released her immediately with a "Sorry," and then, "I'll be right back."

Eleanor watched him, amazed when he tore after the culprit who'd snatched her bag. She hadn't really gotten a good look at her savior, but she'd heard his low, Irish-accented melodious voice.

She leaned back against the wall of a men's haberdashery and waited as several people stopped to ask if she was all right. Heat bloomed in her cheeks at the fuss they made over her and she told them she was fine, and that someone was looking after her. Two elderly ladies and a man stood with her as she waited for the man who'd taken off after the thief to return.

Then she groaned at the sight of the run in her silk stocking. She supposed it didn't matter for she wouldn't be returning to St. Paul soon, and she never wore dresses at the resort.

The tall, muscular man appeared again and strode toward her. She was relieved to see he had her bag in his hand. He stopped in front of her with a big smile, his white, even teeth sparkling in the light of day. Then he thanked the people who'd stayed with her and they left.

He handed over her purse. "Here you go."

Then, looking around a moment, he turned to her with a frown. "You walking the streets alone then?" At her slight nod, he said, "You really shouldn't. Things are hard for folks right now. And your purse was too much temptation for that boy."

Again, that silky Irish voice reached her ears and she felt her body go limp. His voice was like music to her ears, which made her wonder if he didn't make sweet music for his livelihood. Looking way up, she met his eyes, an unusual topaz color, saw his curling hair the color of rich mahogany. She caught the worried expression on his face and set out to calm his fears, wondering at the same time why he worried about her welfare when they didn't know each other.

Self-conscious now, she straightened her hat and tucked her hair behind her ears, glancing surreptitiously at him. He was half a foot taller than she was and built like the lumbermen she'd seen along the St. Croix River cutting down trees.

"You want to call the police and press charges?"

Her eyes widened on him as she pulled herself up straight and sidestepped away from him. "Why, I don't think so. Besides, I don't know the boy, and he's likely far away from here by now."

"I know him, but I don't know if I should give you his name or not."

"Why not?" she asked, suddenly growing angry about the assault, now that she'd recovered. "He could have really hurt me."

"Not Peter. He's got a drunkard dad, and a mom who took sick and to her bed months ago. Peter's the sole supporter of his family, which includes four younger brothers." Looking around, he leaned down and said softly, "It's hard enough for a grown man to find work, let alone a fourteen-year-old boy."

Her anger dimmed then, and her heart softened as she nodded. "You're right, of course. When you speak with the boy, tell him he could have asked me for coin and I would have helped him."

The man grinned. "I certainly will tell him that." He tipped his hat then and stood there, smiling down at her until she grew uncomfortable. Then she thought about his words, "drunken father."

"Wait a minute. You said his father was a drunkard?" At the man's nod, she added, "But we've been in Prohibition for the past several years."

"Ma'am, there's ways a man can find a drink if he needs it—craves it—like Peter's father does."

She sighed. "I suppose you're right. Well, thank you for helping me."

"You're welcome. Now how about I escort you home?"

"I don't live in St. Paul, but I'm staying at my brother's place."

"Then I'll walk you the rest of the way."

As he took her elbow and walked her down the street, heading past shops and cafes, she chattered nervously. He simply smiled, listened, and nodded now and then to something she said, but didn't talk much. In a way, his quiet manner intrigued her, especially since her brother talked incessantly. Soon she quieted as well, feeling self-conscious by his silence.

They turned on Arbor Street and she stopped at the foot of the steps leading up to a two-story brick home. She stuck out her hand. "I can't thank you enough for coming to my rescue." He took her hand and squeezed it gently, his gaze searching hers.

"No problem, ma'am."

"Well, then, I'd better let you return to your work." She turned away and took the first two steps up when he spoke.

"Don't have any work right now."

She whirled around and took him in from head to toe. He wore dungarees, a long-sleeved chambray shirt with a flannel wool plaid jacket over it, and boots with worn toes on his feet. The newspaper boy's hat he wore tilted jauntily on his head. Suspenders held up his dungarees and Eleanor found herself gazing upon his broad chest and strong muscular arms beneath the long sleeves of his shirt; strong arms that could easily, she imagined, swing a hammer, and pound a few nails…

"Mister…."

"Riley Flaherty, ma'am."

"I'm Eleanor Swenson," she said with a nod, "so stop calling me ma'am. How would you like a job?"

Riley pulled his steamer trunk from beneath his bed at the lumbermen's crew house where he'd lived for the past seven years. Everything he owned fit into that trunk, and as he folded his clothes neatly inside, excitement flared through him, which was something; he hadn't felt excited about much for a long time.

He hummed a song as he thought about the pretty Swedish girl he'd be working for—Eleanor Swenson. A lovely name for a lovely young woman. He tried to imagine her living alone last year in her wilderness home and couldn't. He had been born and raised in a bustling city and wasn't so sure he could take the solitude, but he was willing to try.

She was tall for a woman, but narrowly built, sweet, and feminine. All he could think was how unprotected she was there, alone, with just a few people renting cabins over a brief time of the year. It just wasn't right for the woman to live there alone, and in his opinion, her brother should have put his foot down, sold the property, and made her stay in St. Paul.

He slammed the lid shut and hoisted the trunk to his shoulder. Then he bent and picked up the handle of the case that held his prized possession, a fine fiddle from his grandfather when Riley left home for America. Riley had had some lessons from his grandfather and had easily learned how to play the instrument. For a short while, upon arriving in America eight years ago, he'd managed to make a living playing the instrument for coin, on the streets—to whoever paid to hear him to play. He'd even secured a month-long run playing his fiddle every night in the Wabasha Street Caves in St. Paul, in one of several speakeasies built into the sandstone caves located on the south shore of the Mississippi River.

As he ran down the steps, he shouted "good-bye" and "good luck" to his fellow lumbermen, ready to embark on an exciting new life for himself. The pay from Eleanor would be only a third of what he'd earned as a "jack" but it didn't matter. Other than a few personal necessities and food, he needed little.

He was a simple man who led a simple but satisfying life. The only thing that hadn't satisfied him was being without a wife and children. While he'd listened to Eleanor talk about Swenson's Haven, he couldn't help imagining her in her modest cabin home, in the midst of a vast wilderness, growing flowers and vegetables, cooking, the wafting scent of freshly baked bread as he entered the kitchen. He imagined himself being married to her and sharing that modest cabin. He imagined her big and round with his child and heat suffused his face at the thought. But then the thought of living away from the bright lights of the city made him feel gloomy. He loved tipping a pint with his fellow workers in the local pubs, and had to admit he'd miss that, but then again, he'd be married to sweet Eleanor who he thought would be perfect for him.

Damn. He was getting way ahead of himself. He had to learn to get to know the lass first. Sure, he'd courted plenty of pretty girls over the years, but upon meeting Eleanor, the memories of them diminished. He just had a feeling that she was "the one."

He sighed then as he strode toward Arbor Street. This was a business arrangement, yet he couldn't see a problem with mixing a bit of pleasure with it. Besides, he remembered her saying how she'd been lonely with no one to talk to all winter long, and his smile widened. She wouldn't be alone this winter for he'd made a full-year commitment to being her handyman.

Riley arrived outside the Swenson family home just as Eleanor was struggling down the steps with a box. He dropped his steamer trunk from his shoulder and eased the box from her hands, astonished by its weight, and that this slip of a girl had managed to carry it. Frowning, he said, "This is way too heavy for you. Where do you want it?"

"Good morning, Riley," she said. "Why, in the back seat of my automobile would be fine.

Riley followed her pointing finger and his eyes widened. She owned an automobile, specifically an American-made Austin Model A coup. "You...drive?" he asked.

"Why, yes. How else would we get to the resort?"

Heat flared in his cheeks again and he murmured, "Thought we were taking a streetcar or train."

She laughed. "Riley? Where we're going there are few forms of transportation. We drive, or we take a small airplane, which I refuse to do."

He stared at her a moment, taking in her long wheat-colored hair worn straight to her waist. God, how he wouldn't love to fist his hands in all of that fine stuff, he mused. His eyes slid to her surprisingly mannish attire, which looked enticing on her; a tan-colored broadcloth shirt that buttoned down the front, with matching tan-colored pants, and practical low-heeled tie shoes on her feet. She wore a red and gold plaid woolen jacket, similar to his own, and held a straw hat in her hand which she brushed against her leg as she met his gaze straight on. He liked that, how she didn't blush and look away.

Riley heard a door slam then and a man who resembled Eleanor raced down the stairs. He clutched a full-length robe around him and wore a scowl on his face. Giving Riley a nod in passing, he stalked over to Eleanor and scowled down at her. "You really are returning to the resort, aren't you?"

"I told you that I was—it's my home now."

He sighed. "You were leaving without saying good-bye."

"It's the crack of dawn and I know how you hate rising early."

"True, but did you think I wouldn't want to say good-bye to my own sister, whom I won't see for who knows how long?"

With that, he pulled her into his arms for a big hug. She hugged him in return and Riley sighed, wiping away ill thoughts of this man being a possible beau.

John released her then and strode over to Riley. He held out his hand and Riley took it. Riley saw John sizing him up, suspicion on his face, but soon he smiled and released his hand. "You appear to be a trustworthy man, Mr. Flaherty. Take care of my sister. You hear?"

"I will, you can count on me," Riley said, his voice firm.

"Have a safe trip, you two!" John called as he raced up the steps and disappeared inside the house, slamming the door in his wake.

Riley looked at Eleanor and she shrugged. "He's glad I've hired you on."

"Uh, don't you think it's unusual how he seems to trust me, a stranger?

"Not at all. He checked you out, including interviewing your previous boss and friends at the lumber mill."

Riley frowned.

"You're not mad about that, are you? As you said, we are strangers and…"

"Your brother did the right thing. It's just that I'm not used to my personal life being invaded, but like I said, I can't blame him."

"Then let's get going, shall we?"

Riley watched her as she walked over to the passenger side of her car and slid inside. He caught a glimpse of a pretty, slim ankle as her pants rode up a bit, then she tucked her legs inside and closed the door. He stood indecisively, riveted in place, his cheeks heating up again.

She opened the door and stood up with a quizzical expression. "What's wrong? Did you forget something?"

"Uh, Miss Swenson? I don't know how to drive."

"Oh!" she gasped. "Sorry," she murmured, a small smile on her lips. "Didn't want to possibly chance bruising your male ego by having you ride with me rather than drive." With a shrug of her shoulders, she left the passenger door open for him and came around to the driver side. As she slid behind the wheel, she said, "None of this Miss Swenson business. It's Eleanor. Let's get going. It'll take us seven to eight hours to get to the resort."

He settled down in the passenger seat and closed the door behind him. He'd wanted an automobile for the past five years but had yet to save up enough money. Maybe she'd let him take it out on the resort property for a spin or two, he mused.

Seeming to read his mind, she said, "I'll teach you how to drive since you'll want to use the vehicle to haul supplies from the storage cabin to the resort cabins you'll be working on. Really, what I should do is get us a truck, but I want to spend my money on renovating the cabins first."

"I understand, and thanks for the offer to teach me. I appreciate it."

The farther north Eleanor drove, the less assured Riley felt about taking the job. As they left the city behind, farmlands being harvested for crops filled the landscape. With miles in between, they passed through several small towns composed of a few shops, mercantiles, and at each place they stopped at a petroleum station and topped off the tank on Eleanor's automobile.

Riley thoroughly enjoyed the hustle and bustle of crowds and city life, especially after working in fair isolation, with just a few other lumbermen for companionship cutting trees in the north woods for several weeks at a time. It appeared Eleanor's home was in the woods and away from any sizeable city. He wondered if he could handle the peace and quiet he expected for an entire rotation of seasons. He'd signed on with her until the end of next summer, nearly a year away.

Eleanor played tour guide and Riley relaxed in his seat as he listened to her talk about the crops on the farms they passed, pointed out the different types of trees and animals along the way. He looked out his passenger side window and lurched forward when she hit the brakes suddenly.

"Be very still and he'll leave the road. We don't want him to possibly charge us," she whispered.

Riley followed her gaze and swore under his breath when he saw an enormous moose standing in the middle of the road, staring at them. After several minutes of waiting, he nudged Eleanor.

"Uh, maybe you should hit the horn."

"No. I've been with my brother when the very same thing happened. He sounded the horn and the moose charged us. Luckily, we were able to go into reverse, and then turned and drove away—swiftly, I might add." She tilted her head to look at the moose critically, and added, "This may be the same moose. We must be in his territory."

At a loss for words, and thinking what he'd gotten himself into, he slouched down in his seat and scowled at the beast who languidly stood, watching, waiting for them to make a move, he suspected. A few minutes later he breathed a relieved sigh when the animal ambled down the road, then veered off and headed into the forest.

"Finally!" Eleanor exclaimed, then put the automobile in gear again and drove away.

The weather had grown noticeably cooler, too, and he hadn't thought to pack more than a medium-weight jacket. He wasn't worried though as Eleanor said they would drive into the town nearest to the resort about once a month, and he could purchase winter gear there.

The sun went lower and he knew it would soon be dark.

"Almost there," Eleanor said.

He heard the enthusiasm in her voice and smiled. She was happy to be home, and her happiness piqued his interest.

After having headed north for several hundred miles, mostly on poorly paved roads, they took a turn east onto a rough dirt road. The automobile rumbled merrily along as she drove while Riley held onto the seat and set his teeth against the jarring motion. After another half hour, they arrived in a small clearing where he counted five small rustic cabins.

Eleanor parked her automobile near one cabin, jumped out and ran around to the passenger side. "Come on!" she called as she swung open his door, "You have to see the lake. It's gorgeous at dusk."

He grinned when she pulled at his hand and he grasped hers and allowed her to pull him out of her automobile and around the log building. She stopped suddenly, before the ground headed down to the lake, and he paused beside her, following her gaze. They looked across a good-sized lake and at the sun as it just started setting. The sky had turned a purple-pink color and Riley's heart pounded wildly as he stared at the magnificent sight. He'd never seen a lake so unencumbered with lights and buildings until now, and the sight mesmerized him.

"Beautiful, isn't it?" she whispered with rightful reverence.

"Like nothing I've ever seen," he murmured.

They stood side by side, holding hands as they watched the sun make its final descent and disappear beneath the horizon. He stared at Eleanor then, saw a hank of pale hair flowing across her face, and without thought, reached out and tucked the strand behind her ear.

She turned then and faced him, her eyes sparkling still, smile in place.

"What did you think?" she asked.

He raised one eyebrow. "About what?"

"The sunset, of course."

"Beautiful." Just like you, darlin'. He saw her cheeks turn pink and then she shivered. "Let's go inside. You're cold."

"Good idea," she said, all businesslike. She strode to the cabin right behind them, pulled on a string latch, which opened the door.

Riley frowned as he followed her inside, closed the door, then stared at the bar across it. Jamming his hands on his hips, he continued glaring at the door.

"What's wrong?"

"You don't have a lock on this door. And what good does this one bar do?"

"Don't need one. We're in the north woods."

He looked at her over his shoulder. "What does being in the woods have to do with safety?"

"We're miles away from civilization," she said as she moved to a small stove where an old tin coffeepot sat. "I don't need to lock the door."

"Don't you have paying guests up here though?"

"Just a few this late in the season. Day after tomorrow I've got some fishermen coming up from Iowa, so I need to clean the cabin they'll be using for the week. Stop fussing. If you feel so strongly about it, you can put a lock on the door later." She grabbed the coffeepot.

A brisk breeze swept through the room. "And there's no insulation in here," he complained. "You're telling me you stayed up here, alone, all last winter?" At her nod, he snapped, "Good grief, woman, how did you plug the holes around the door, not to mention the holes between the logs?"

"I stuffed socks, fabric, weeds, hay—whatever I could find to close me in, that's how."

"Don't tell me you were all snug and warm. I won't believe it."

"I won't tell you, but I did survive," she said, tilting her nose in the air. Then she opened the door.

"Where are you off to?"

"I'm making coffee and the water's in the pump outside."

His arm came out and he stopped her from leaving. "I'll get it."

She relinquished the pot to him. "All right, thanks."

Eleanor smiled when she heard Riley mutter softly, "First thing we'll do is install indoor plumbing." That would be fine with her. Once the snow came and temperatures dropped, she couldn't pump water anymore, but had resorted last winter to bringing in pails of snow and melting it over the stove.

While she busied herself pulling a few potatoes and onions out of a bin, she frowned as she reached the bottom. A week ago, before she left for St. Paul, the bin had been filled to its limit with vegetables from her garden she'd harvested, but it was near empty now. Then she heard Riley's roar outside and she rushed to the door. Just as she reached to open it, the door slammed open and Riley raced inside, soaking wet. Whirling around, he slammed the door behind him and braced his arms and legs hard against the wooden portal.

"What happened?"

"Bear," he gasped.

Eleanor raced to the window and peered between the curtains. Sure enough, there was a medium-sized black bear, headed straight for the cabin.

"Damn, he's following me." Riley glared at her. "This is why we need a lock on the door."

She scoffed, "You can't mean to tell me you think a bear will try and come inside, do you?"

Eleanor stilled at the sound of scratching against the wood. Her eyes widened in horror when the bar started to lift then fell down with a clap. They rushed forward, bumping into each other until Riley pushed her aside. She paused and watched him as he leaned his body weight against the door, then shrieked in dismay when the door started to open. He pressed himself firmly against it until it slammed shut once more.

"What are we going to do?" she wailed.

Riley peered around the room and his eyes lit upon a heavy wood table. "Come over here and lean against the door."

"Me! Why, I weigh far less than you do."

He smirked. "I know that. But if we want to keep this bear out, we need to shove something heavy against the door. And the only thing I figure that will work is the table."

Without a word, Eleanor raced over and traded places with Riley, jamming her back against the door and digging in her heels.

Thank heavens Riley moved swiftly for he managed to shove the table in front of the door before the bear made his way inside, though Eleanor felt the door give several times as she held her weight against the bear's strength.

They both heaved sighs of relief when they heard the bear's high-pitched complaints then silence. They straightened up, released their combined weights from the table's edge, and peered out the window again. They saw the bear lumbering away and disappear into the forest.

"Okay, you were right," Eleanor said. "That bear's been inside the cabin before."

"How do you know?"

"Cause my vegetable bin is near empty and I'd filled it with vegetables from my garden before I left for St. Paul."

Riley frowned. "Doesn't the bin have a cover?"

"Sure, a hinged one, which I probably left wide open." She sighed, and then looked into his eyes—very blue eyes that sparkled with humor.

"You think this is funny, don't you?" she said indignantly.

"No. But you are one sweet colleen, Miss Eleanor," he breathed softly.

Eleanor widened her eyes as he leaned down to her, his gaze now focused on her lips.

He was going to kiss her. She knew she should turn away from him, but she couldn't. His eyes were mesmerizing as they stayed focused on her lips. Male scents surrounded her; his tangy shaving cream, the wool scent of his shirt, a tiny waft of tobacco, though she hadn't seen him smoking or chewing any. She remained utterly still.

Eleanor started to shove the table, intent upon moving it back to its original place, but Riley stopped her. "We're leaving that table right where it is until I install a lock tomorrow."

She paused and swiped a lock of hair off her forehead. "I suppose you're right."

"Have bears tried coming in here in the past?"

"Inside? No, but I've seen them on the property before, this past spring. I guess they didn't realize I was here then." She gnawed on her lower lip a moment then added, "But I'm thinking it's getting closer to winter and the bears are likely looking for food before they go into hibernation."

"You're probably right. But weren't you here last autumn and winter?"

"I didn't arrive until late November, and after the first snowfall. I didn't see any bears until mid-March."

"Makes sense," Riley said, giving a decisive nod. "But we're here earlier this time. I'll just feel a lot better once I insulate this place and put on a lock."

"Me too." She tilted her head and smiled at him. "Thanks for being here."

"Don't thank me yet. I'm having some doubts about signing up with you. I might just change my mind and leave you here."

Eleanor grinned at his scowling visage. "And I don't blame you, I guess. But then, you said you don't have any work to return home to, so why not stay? I've a feeling we've a true north woods adventure ahead of us."

"Kiddo, your sense of adventure could be the death of us," he groaned. "Not only am I picking up a lock tomorrow, but a gun wouldn't hurt."

⚜

The next day, Eleanor and Riley drove to the nearest town of Orting—tiny at eighty people—to the only hardware store in the vicinity. Riley purchased a lock for the cabin's front door, and several heavy-duty woolen blankets he planned to cut into strips he'd use to insulate the cabin. He also, upon guidance from the shopkeeper, bought a long-range Hauser game rifle and several boxes of ammunition.

Eleanor stood beside him at the store and paid for the items herself, except for the gun and ammunition. As Riley paid, she shuddered. "Don't expect me to learn to use it. I hate guns!"

He slanted a smile at her. "Wasn't expecting to teach you. The kick from this gun would land you on your—"

"You don't need to tell me," she snapped. "Do you know how to shoot it?"

He gave a brief nod but didn't meet her eyes. She had a feeling he knew all about guns, just from how he handled it, sighted down the length of it.

Eleanor purchased some extra food provisions, gassed up her automobile, and headed back to the resort. While she drove, she smiled, thinking how embarrassed Riley seemed last night, sharing the cabin with her. She wondered how a big, handsome man like Riley could feel self-conscious around her. Shouldn't it be the other way around? She hadn't been self-conscious or uncomfortable sharing her cabin with a virtual stranger. Her smile slipped. Maybe she should have been, but then she shrugged. She enjoyed having company in the form of Riley Flaherty and looked forward to spending a cozy winter with him. He'd insisted on taking the single bed in the small, second bedroom while Eleanor slept in her own big bed. Alone.

Eleanor hadn't much experience with men but had been courted enough to know a good man from a bad one. Her instincts about people had always been good and she had a good feeling about Riley.

With just a few miles to home, Eleanor decided it was the perfect time for Riley to learn to drive. She pulled over to the side of the road and stopped the automobile. Opening her door, she jumped out, crossed the front of the automobile, and stood at the passenger side.

He'd raised his eyebrows as he sat slumped in his seat. "We stopping for a reason?"

"You're going to drive. If something happened to me, you'd be stuck up here."

Eagerness crossed his face as he hopped out of the automobile and raced around to the driver's side. She settled into the passenger seat and nearly laughed aloud when she saw him clutching the wheel, his head ducking down to check out the automobile's gauges. The awed look in his eyes made her think of a child opening presents on Christmas.

"So, how come you never learned to drive?"

"Been planning on buying one of these the last couple of years but have never been in a rush to since the company drives us to our cutting jobs. Haven't really had a need for one. And I've been saving my money for other more important things."

"Like what?"

"A home of my own, for one thing. I've sort of outgrown living in the bunkhouse with the other lumbermen. Need my own place."

She nodded. "Yes, I couldn't imagine cohabitating with several people. I enjoy my privacy and solitude—to a point."

He grinned and held onto the steering wheel. "But you let me in your door, though. Why?"

"I really do need a handyman to help me at the resort if I want to grow the business. And I know my limits as to what I can and can't do."

"How many other men had you asked?"

"Actually, I'd come down to St. Paul to beg my brother to return with me. Other than him, you're the only one."

He frowned. "You always make it a habit to approach strange men?"

"Never. This was the first time." She laughed.

"I wouldn't advise doing so again," he warned.

"Remember? I said my brother had you investigated and deemed you safe. And now I won't have to find another handyman, will I?"

He nodded then said dryly, "Give me some pointers."

"Well, there's really little to do." She explained to him how to start the automobile, put it into gear, how to press on the pedals to go and stop it, and how to work the clutch to change gears. He proceeded cautiously, but not for long. Soon he drove along with ease.

Eleanor was amazed and impressed. It had taken her a year to learn how to drive and shift the gears without thinking about it so much—until it became second nature.

After several miles, she praised him. "You're doing great! Now, would you like me to take over for a while?"

"No. I need more practice."

She laughed, then wondered what other talents he possessed. The man had learned to drive from the moment he got into the driver's seat—a natural, guess you could say. She sank back and for a change enjoyed the scenery, even though the road was rough and bumpy.

Once they arrived at the resort, they unloaded their supplies. Riley started out immediately cutting the blankets into strips and pressing it between the logs where he saw daylight. Eleanor pulled cheese out of the icebox, then opened the big pantry in the kitchen, found bread and made simple cheese sandwiches and cups of cold soup since they were too hungry to wait for the oven to heat up once she placed wood inside. Afterward, she gathered her cleaning supplies and fresh bedding. As she headed out of the cabin, she said, "I'll be at Owl's Nest."

He looked up with a confused expression. "Owl's Nest?"

She grinned. "The cabin just up the road a bit. My parents named the cabins."

"Why Owl's Nest?"

"'Cause it sits on a high hill. My fishermen will be using that cabin so I'm getting it ready."

"What's the name of this cabin?"

"Home Sweet Home."

"Ah, good name, but I didn't see any sign on the cabin saying so."

"I've been meaning to have some made—haven't had the chance yet."

"I can do that for you."

"Wonderful! There's an engraver in town that can do it. And he thankfully doesn't charge a fortune."

"No charge since I can make the signs and do the engraving too."

"Oh, you know how to engrave?"

"Sure do. Even have my own wood tools with me."

She grinned. "I just had a feeling you'd be a good handyman, but engraving is an art. You are multitalented, Riley."

"Thanks," he murmured, not meeting her eyes.

Her grin widened when she saw his cheeks and neck turn pink. Apparently, the man wasn't used to compliments. She made up her mind then to pay him as many as she could. Then guilt plagued her; she'd hired him for much less, she was certain, than what he'd been paid as a lumberman. She prayed he'd stay the one full year to which he committed.

She went around back of the cabin and returned pulling an old wagon behind her. She entered her cabin again and picked up soap and vinegar she'd wrapped in towels and carried them to the wagon.

"Let me help you," Riley said from the open door.

"Thanks," she murmured, grateful for his assistance.

He left the house with his arms piled high with bedding and plopped them into the wagon. "You sure you can handle that load?"

"Sure. No problem."

"I'll go with you," he insisted.

"No, I'm fine on my own. Besides, winter will be setting in soon so it's important that you get that chinking done. It'll take you a while."

"All right, but don't be afraid to call me for help if you need it."

"Okay." She turned away, pulled on the handle, and trudged up the road. She reached a dirt drive and turned right, walking toward the Owl's Nest, tucked neatly into the woods. As she neared the front door she frowned when she saw the door wide open and flapping in the breeze.

She paused a distance away and looked keenly around the cabin but saw no sign of human or animal. Maybe the latch had broken after the last patrons left at the end of summer. She hadn't been in any of the cabins for over a month and decided she'd better check the other three as well once she'd cleaned this one.

Cautiously, broom in hand, she moved toward the front door. She peeked inside then jerked back when she saw movement close to the ground. Gulping down the growing lump in her throat she gathered her courage, took another step, and peered inside. The cabin's first room was the kitchen-living area.

A large furry animal appeared, and she shrieked to the heavens as he ran toward her. She propelled backward, stumbling to get away from the fleeing animal. The thing rushed up and past her, bumping hard against her pants leg and prickly pain seared her skin. The air around her reeked of an ammonia scent and she realized what her furry friend was—a skunk!

She heard pounding, running footsteps behind her and she whirled around to see Riley. The first thing that entered her mind was how swiftly he ran for a big man. He stopped beside her and pulled her against his chest.

Eleanor hadn't realized tears were slipping down her cheeks until he reached down and swiped one away.

"Damn! Did that skunk get you?"

"Unfortunately, yes, and the nearest doctor is twenty-two miles away."

Riley looked down at her pants leg and gulped. "You're bleeding."

She looked down then and nearly fainted for blood was seeping out slowly through her heavy pants, from her calf. The pain seemed to worsen after that.

"Let's get you back to the cabin," he said, guiding her with an arm around her waist.

After only limping a few steps, she whispered, "Wait a minute. I think I'm going to pass—"

"Out," he finished and swept her up in his arms.

That was the last thing Eleanor remembered until she awoke on her bed. Riley stood over her, unbuckling her belt.

She stayed utterly still when she realized he planned on removing her pants. Breathing softly, she watched him from beneath half-slit eyes. His touch was firm yet gentle, and she quivered in anticipation of what he'd do; wondered how far he'd go. After all, if her simple compliments could cause him to blush, she imagined he'd be redder than an apple if he undressed her.

Eleanor knew she should let him know she was conscious, but she couldn't resist pretending. No man had ever touched her as intimately as Riley, and she craved to know what it felt like to be truly loved by a man.

No man, thus far, had ever gone this far with her for she hadn't been ready for it; hadn't been attracted enough, she supposed. But Riley attracted her plenty.

Riley's hands paused on Eleanor's belt. Damn. He'd undressed a few women in his time, but those women allowed any man to undress them for a price. He'd never undressed a decent woman, but then, a decent woman wouldn't allow a man that privilege, unless the two of them were married.

But this was a medical emergency and a necessity.

He pulled the notch open then slipped his hands beneath her, found the back of her pants, and started to tug them down, lifting her a bit to free the fabric. He frowned, thinking he was imagining things; did her hips rise up because of him, or because of her? Was it possible she was playing "possum" with him? He paused with his hands still on her waistband, pants pulled down to her thighs as he stared at her face.

No. He shook his head. She was out cold, so he hurried to finish the job. Once he'd pulled her pants all the way off he grimaced at the prickly holes in her calf. Damn. The critter had done a number on her. Prone to faint-heartedness upon the sight of blood, Riley knew she needed him now, so he managed to remain calm and conscious.

Eleanor opened her eyes after she felt him move away. Her gaze followed him as he strode over to a kitchen cupboard and removed some items. He returned to her then and she decided she couldn't pretend anymore.

Riley heaved a relieved sigh when he made eye contact with her. "Glad you've returned, ma'am."

Eleanor choked back a laugh as his gaze swept down her body, over her white cotton underwear and bare thighs. She raised her gaze to his. "I think we've passed the *ma'am* stage, Riley."

There it was again—that cute blush on his face, but no reply.

She laughed. "No need to be embarrassed. There might come a time when I'll need to undress you."

"Eleanor, stop it," he said roughly. "You're hurt so how can you make jokes?"

Feeling chastened, Eleanor frowned and felt heat seep into her cheeks. She sat up on her bed and looked in dismay at her calf. "That old skunk sure as all get out stuck me, didn't he?"

"Yea, lass, he sure did. The answer to any wound is cleansing, so grit your teeth and hold still. You might want to not look so why don't you lie down again."

Eleanor complied and cringed, tears filling her eyes when he cleaned the wounds with soap and water he'd retrieved from the kitchen. She felt him pat it dry and started to sit up when he pressed on her shoulder with one hand.

"I'm not done yet. So, this next step will burn like hell, but it's necessary."

He held up a bottle of some brown liquid—antiseptic—he found in the cupboard.

Before Eleanor could even think to pull away or tell him no, he splashed the brownish liquid onto her leg. She shrieked and grabbed his wrist, preventing him from pouring it again. "Are you crazy? Why didn't you give me a chance to prepare!" she wailed.

"If I gave you a chance to think about it, you wouldn't have allowed me to do it. Now hold still, clutch the bedding, or something," he murmured as he went about dabbing at the wounds with a clean cloth, sopping up the dripping antiseptic.

Tears filled Eleanor's eyes at the sting, but she remained rigid, knowing the ordeal would soon be over. Once he'd bandaged her leg up she felt a bit better, even though her wounds felt as if they'd been scrubbed with a brush.

"I want you to stay in bed."

"You know I can't," she protested as she squirmed to sit up. "I've got those fishermen coming in tomorrow."

"I'll change the beds and clean up the place. You stay put."

"Oh, Riley, she groaned. "That's not why I hired you."

"Sure it is. I'll do anything that needs doing around here. Now stay in bed. I'll be back to make us something to eat in a bit."

She felt her lower lip tremble and her voice as well. "You're so good to me. Thank you."

He smiled. "You're welcome. No thanks necessary, though. I know you'd do the same for me."

She went on to explain to him exactly what needed to be done with the other cabins.

❦

Riley locked the cabin door and left, garden rake and rifle in hand, glad he knew how to use the weapon.

He'd grown up in the big city of Dublin in Ireland, and crime was rampant. Wherever there was poverty, it seemed that way. Therefore, from a young age, his father had taught him how to load, aim, and shoot a gun. His aim had always been good. Luckily, he'd only had to use a gun a few times before he left Ireland, seeking work opportunities in America. Sure, he could have taken over his father's grocery store business, but he'd hated being stuck inside all day. He wanted to feel the sun on his body, warm summer breezes, even the snow in winter, and Minnesota provided him all of those things.

He cleaned up the Owl's Nest, then moved onto the other three cabins. After removing bedding, cleaning out cupboards and readying them for winter, the job took up most of his day. Only Home Sweet Home would be winter-hardy. From what Eleanor had told him, they'd be spending the winter chopping wood, winterizing the cabin, and making repairs, including building on two more bedrooms.

After she'd explained her ambitious plans, he was embarrassed to tell her that he didn't know much about building but could repair things that were already made. She said she had another couple men coming in to build the addition onto the cabin and he could be of the most use to them in cutting down the trees necessary for the project. He'd been happy to hear that and confident that he could do the job since cutting was his line of work.

When he returned to the cabin, he found Eleanor asleep on her bed and closed the door softly.

He started in on insulating the cabin and when it grew too dark to work, day turning into evening, he stopped. He peeked into Eleanor's room and found her asleep still and he wondered if maybe he shouldn't wake her. Deciding against it, he went outside to fetch some of the firewood he'd chopped that morning.

The cabin had two fireplaces, and he shivered when he thought how those were the only source of heat for a long winter. The insulation he'd installed would help, but next time they went to town, he'd talk with the few shopkeepers to see how they kept their homes warm. Maybe he could install some sort of heating system, other than depending on firewood.

Once he loaded up the woodbin, he turned to the kitchen. His stomach had been rumbling for the past hour. Jamming his hands on his hips he sighed. He was awful in a kitchen, having never had to cook for himself. His mum had in Ireland, his sisters too, and at his lumber job the company provided all meals.

Eleanor was in no condition to cook so he peered inside her small icebox, found ground meat of some kind, and pulled it out, noting though the block of ice was nearly gone. Tomorrow he'd run into town and pick up another block. The meat had been wrapped in white butcher paper, and now, as he stared at the hunk of meat, wondering how to prepare it, he wished he'd thought of pulling it out earlier.

"Hi."

He whirled around and found Eleanor standing in the kitchen entrance. She smiled at him and she looked sleepy though more alert than she had earlier that day. She'd dressed in her tan trousers and shirt and wore slippers on her feet.

"Why aren't you in bed?"

His scowl nearly made her laugh aloud. "'Cause I'm feeling better and my stomach's growling, feed me, feed me."

"Mine too. I just found this meat in the ice chest and was trying to figure out what to do with it. Uh, any idea what kind of meat it is?"

"Moose."

"You're joking."

Now she laughed. "Nope, I'm not. One of the neighbors on the lake gave it to me. Just haven't had a chance to cook it yet. With just me here all winter last year, I kept things quick and simple.

"Why don't you take a chair and I'll cook this up in a pan?"

"I don't feel like moose meat, but bacon and eggs I could handle. You sit down. I know you've worked all day and I'm feeling better."

He protested, mildly, but gave in and sank down into a chair at the table and resumed cutting strips of the blankets to use for insulation.

He watched Eleanor as she returned the moose meat to the icebox. Then she lit the wood in the stove, and returned to the icebox where she pulled out thick-cut bacon and eggs.

Riley admired how sweet she looked as she efficiently and quickly prepared them food. She toasted some thick slices of bread in a cast iron skillet. Then she cooked half of the bacon and fried up six eggs. She set the coffeepot to percolating on the stove, then pulled a jar of orange marmalade jam out of the pantry and set it on the table, along with dishes and silverware.

Soon they sat and started to eat, speaking little. Riley was so hungry he cleaned up his plate in record time.

Without a word, he watched Eleanor rise from her chair, fry up two more eggs, and brown more toast for him. He gave her a grateful look when she slid the eggs and toast onto his plate. While he ate, she drank her coffee and watched him. Somehow, the feeling of her eyes on him made him feel wanted, needed, and he liked that—a lot.

He sank back in his chair, his hunger satisfied, then felt self-conscious. He sensed her eyes on him still, and suddenly he was embarrassed by his worn, brown flannel shirt, and old dungarees with suspenders. He raised his eyes, half-slit now as lethargy stole over him. He took in his fill of her, devoured her. He smiled slightly when he saw her skin pinken and she bit her lower lip.

"It's going to be a long winter," he murmured, and he sank against the back of his chair.

"They're all long, I'm afraid."

He heard the tremble in her voice and saw her clasp her hands tightly in her lap. He frowned, wondering at her skittishness. Then he thought about the long winter ahead, sharing a cabin with her.

"I'm talking real long, unless…"

"Unless?" she whispered.

Riley's gaze traveled over her hair, her lips, down her throat and over her chest. He knew she understood him, and he saw the look in her eyes that told him she wanted him every bit as much as he wanted her. If they were meant to be for just this one year... Still, he hesitated.

"Unless?" she asked again as she slowly rose from the table and came around it. He didn't reply but heat tore through him as he looked up at her standing beside him now. She reached down and fingered a lock of his hair, twirling it around her finger.

He took her hand in his. "Do you understand what I'm saying?"

❧

Eleanor started to nod saw a look in his eyes that frightened yet thrilled her at the same time. "I...I think so."

He stood up and shook his head. "No, you don't, or you wouldn't have stumbled over your words. You're an innocent young woman and I'm beginning to think, unless you're positively certain you want to be my woman, I'll need to bunk down in one of the other cabins."

"Oh! You can't. Not a one is winter-ready."

"Then before winter settles in I'd better make sure one of them is, hadn't I?"

She didn't reply but nodded as she tried to disguise what she knew was a forlorn expression on her face.

"It's late," he said abruptly. "I'm turning in."

"But..."

"Yes?" he inquired.

Eleanor had enjoyed the company of men in the past, but this feeling inside her was new and frightening and heavenly—all at the same time—yet she knew he was right; she wasn't ready for this kind of...passion.

When she didn't reply, he said, "Like I said, I'm turning in."

He started heading for the front door, ready to leave the cabin.

"Where are you going?"

"To the cabin next door. I'll be fine there during the next month or so."

Tears filled her eyes, yet she nodded. "All right, but tonight you can still sleep in the extra bedroom."

"Thank you, ma'am. I appreciate it."

She sighed as she watched him stride out of the kitchen to the small bedroom down the short hallway. So he'd returned to the formalities again, she mused. But what could she do? She couldn't blame him for wanting to sleep in a separate cabin, knowing the nature of man in general. It wouldn't be fair to put temptation so close. After the fishermen left in a week, she'd help him make one of the other cabins winter-ready for him, so he wouldn't freeze to death.

It had been one very long day—for both of them.

❧

Eleanor woke up the next morning before dawn. As she stumbled out of her tiny bedroom, fully dressed and ready to make breakfast for her and Riley, she moved quietly into the kitchen area. The sun was just starting to rise, the narrow stream of rays illuminating the kitchen area of the cabin. She moved as quietly as she could. Then she heard footsteps on the stairs outside and breathed a relieved sigh when Riley opened the door and strode inside, his arms filled with firewood.

'Mornin'," he said with a nod and headed for the hearth. He

dumped the wood into the bin and slapped his hands together. "You feeling better?"

"Yes, much. Thanks for all of your help yesterday. I shudder to think what I would have done if I'd been by myself."

He shrugged. "You were here last year all by yourself. You probably would have managed fine."

To her mind, she hadn't managed well, which was why she'd come looking for a handyman. She'd been miserable and cold, barely able to sleep at night, even with a fire going. With Riley here, this winter would be much better. It couldn't get any worse, she mused dryly.

Eleanor made breakfast for the two of them. They had just finished eating when she heard the sound of tires on the dirt road.

"Guess that means the fishermen have arrived," Riley said as he rose from his chair. "I'll go out and direct them to the Owl's Nest."

"I'll come with you. This is the same group I had last year. If I don't come out, they'll come in here looking to talk to me. Besides, I'll likely be feeding them breakfast, too."

Outside, three men disembarked from a vehicle that had lost its wax shine miles ago. One of the men, old enough to be Eleanor's father, grinned and stepped over to her, swiping his hat from his head.

"Why, Miss Eleanor, you are a sight for these sore old eyes! How ya been?"

Eleanor grinned, reached out, and took his extended hand. "Just fine, thank you, Mr. Simmons."

With a sly glance at Riley, the old man said, "See ya got yerself hitched over the past year." Heat suffused Eleanor's cheeks and she opened her mouth to reply when Riley stopped her.

"She sure did," Riley said smoothly, taking her hand, and pulling her against his side. "Took me right into the family business and put me to work too," he said with a boisterous laugh.

Which set all three of the men laughing.

Eleanor was stunned by Riley's words. What game was he playing?

"Come on," Riley invited. "Follow me up to your cabin while Eleanor makes you some breakfast."

"Magical words you've said, boy. We love Eleanor's cooking."

Eleanor set to work cooking eggs, hash, bacon, and corn bread. Within moments, the men returned; two sat down at the table and the third sat on the divan. Soon the food was ready, and Eleanor filled their plates.

Soon, only the sound of chewing and scraping of forks against plates could be heard.

Eleanor smiled as she watched the men finish their food, then Mr. Simmons rose. "Thank you, Miz Eleanor. Let's go hit the lake, boys." He grinned at Eleanor. "Maybe we'll be lucky to catch some supper for all of us. How's that sound?"

"Sounds wonderful," Eleanor said. "As long as you all clean those fish before I cook them up."

Riley ambled over to the door and opened it, standing aside to let the men pass by.

"Sure thing, ma'am," said the one man Eleanor didn't know as he stood beside the table.

He'd hardly spoken a word, but he didn't need to speak; the dark sneer on his face made her uncomfortable. She didn't trust him. She turned to Riley and caught him studying the man, his body seemingly relaxed where he leaned against the doorjamb. Yet she had a feeling, from the hard look in his eyes and the set of his jaw that he was far from relaxed.

Mr. Simmons and the other man named Steve Jackson had already left.

A loud bang drew Eleanor's attention. Riley had apparently

slammed the door shut but now opened it. "Better leave, or you'll miss the boat."

The man gave a lethargic shrug. "I'm not much for fishing. I'd much rather stay right here. Maybe Miz Eleanor here needs help with kitchen cleanup."

"Oh, why…" Eleanor started, but stopped when Riley strode toward the man.

Stopping directly in front of him, he met the man's eyes with a glare. "Misses Flaherty has her husband to help her cleanup. Now get going."

The man smirked and jerked his head at Eleanor. "Don't see no ring on her finger. What husband don't even buy his wife a wedding ring?" he asked, his eyes sweeping Eleanor head to toe.

Riley's anger got the best of him. He grabbed the man by the back of the shirt and scuttled him across the floor and out the open door.

A shout of pain filled the morning air and Eleanor gasped, "Riley! Why, you can't treat the paying guests that way!" She raced around Riley and came to a skidding halt when she saw the fisherman picking himself up out of the dirt, grumbling. The man stared daggers at Riley before stalking down to the lake.

Eleanor whirled around and snapped, "What were you thinking? I could lose business because of what you did!"

Riley leaned down, nearly nose to nose with her. "You're angry with me because I protected you?"

"I don't need protection. I lived up here by myself all last winter and did fine, thank you very much." She sniffed.

"Uh-huh. I see how you did. This place is in a shambled condition. This house isn't fit to live in for the winter months. And you've got a hell of a lot of work, lady, in order to make it habitable. Now, then, you either want me to stay and help you or you don't. You wanted a handyman, you said," he reminded her.

"I did—do. But you're behaving like you're my own personal bodyguard. I don't need one, never have. And why did you tell them we're married?"

"The man doesn't respect you. He could have harmed you, maybe tried to...have his way with you, for Christ's sake. You think I could stand by and let that happen?"

She felt heat seep into her cheeks. He had a point. Yet, somehow, she hadn't felt threatened by the fisherman. But then, was it because Riley was with her? She chewed on her lower lip even as tears filled her eyes. "You're right," she said softly. "I didn't feel threatened 'cause you were here. If I'd been by myself, I guess I would have felt differently." She nodded. "Thank you, Riley."

"You're welcome," he said grouchily. He strode inside the cabin and picked up a bucket by its handle.

Eleanor saw screwdrivers, hammers, and the like in the bucket and asked, "Where are you going?"

"To finish up things at one of the cabins. I'll be back in a couple hours."

Eleanor watched him leave and when he disappeared down the road she heaved a sigh. He'd made his point, and while she hadn't liked his high-handed attitude, she had appreciated his being here.

She made moose hash for that evening's supper, cooking the ground-up moose meat in a fry pan with onions, garlic, herbs, and added diced potatoes and carrots. She covered the kettle with a tight cover on one of the wooden stove's burners and went to make the beds. Then she washed the dishes from breakfast. She continued where Riley left off; cutting strips of woolen blanket and shoving them in between the logs. Soon the moose hash was done, and she took it off the burner and left it, ready for supper.

Eleanor left the cabin, then walked up the road to the Owl's Nest to see if she'd forgotten anything for the fishermen. She arrived at the cabin and saw that everything was in its place, wooden floors were clean, beds were made, and the cabin ready for her guests. She saw their luggage had been tossed on the floor in the corner of the two bedrooms and she smiled. Fishing was a priority to these men, not unpacking.

She left the cabin, blankets in hand, and headed next door where she heard Riley at work, pounding away at something. Lover's Lane cabin was tiny, meant for two—a very cozy honeymoon couple cabin. Stepping across the lawn she reached the steps and found Riley just inside the front door, pounding a nail into a piece of wood trim.

"What are you fixing?" she asked.

"Ow! Damn."

Eleanor gasped when the hammer clattered to the floor. He'd hit a finger.

He didn't look at her but rubbed and squeezed the injured appendage.

"Let me look at it."

"No," he said, not looking at her. "It's fine." Now he did lift his eyes to hers. "Don't sneak up on me like that and I won't hurt myself."

Eleanor felt heat seep into her cheeks and she murmured, "Sorry, I didn't even think…what are you fixing?"

He took up the hammer again. "The molding around the door frame was loose so I just tightened it up some."

Eleanor nodded. "Thank you. I noticed that earlier and had placed it on my mental list to fix." Tilting her head to one side, she added, "I don't know if anyone else would have been so observant, though. I brought more blankets to cut up into strips. Maybe I'll start working on this cabin, filling in those holes while you finish your work. Is that okay?" she asked, hesitating when she saw the intense stare he gave her.

She was relieved when a slow grin spread across his lips. "I'd appreciate the company."

With a laugh, Eleanor said, "You'll get used to the quiet soon enough. Then it'll be an adjustment for you when you return to the city. You'll see."

They worked companionably together for several hours, until little daylight remained. As they walked back to their cabin, they saw a fire had been set in one of the pits by the water's edge. The fishermen had returned and as Eleanor and Riley drew up alongside them, she caught the odor of cooking fish.

"That smells heavenly," Eleanor said as she paused beside the fire.

The fishermen were seated on tree stumps they'd rolled down to the pit and with metal plates and forks in hand were digging into crisp fried fish.

"Best walleye fishing ever, Miz Eleanor," Mr. Simmons said. "You're welcome to join us," he added. "We've got plenty."

"Oh, why, thank you, but we'll pass. I've supper ready in the house. Good luck in the morning!" she said as she turned and made her way up the embankment to the cabin, Riley following her.

Inside, she served up corn bread and the moose hash. She laughed aloud when she saw the hesitancy in Riley as he frowned down at a spoonful of hash.

"I guarantee you'll be surprised at the first bite," she announced.

He raised his eyebrows. "As in surprised good or surprised bad?"

"Try it and see."

"Ladies first.

"Oh, my, you really don't trust my cooking, do you?"

"Not true. Your eggs and bacon were great. But, well, eating an innocent wild animal like moose is another story."

"So you've never hunted before?" she asked.

"Small things like rabbit, squirrel, a deer or two, but not moose."

"All right, watch this…" She dug into the hash with her fork and slid it inside her mouth, murmuring delightful sounds and closing her eyes in ecstasy. Then she opened her eyes to see him looking at her suspiciously. She laughed again and took another bite.

She heard him sigh as she savored the hash, then watched him as he tentatively slid a bit off his fork into his mouth. His eyes widened, and he said, "Darn, if that isn't the best thing I've ever tasted! Geez, I think I could get used to this—every day."

Eleanor sat back and took delight in watching him clean his plate then ask her for seconds. After supper, Riley insisted on helping her clean up.

They laughed and talked and laughed more and learned about each other.

When they finished, Eleanor dried her hands on a dishcloth, strolled over to the window at the front of the cabin, and gasped at the sight before her eyes. "Come here, Riley. Look!"

He joined her. "Jeepers, what is that?"

"Aurora Borealis."

"Thought you could only see them in Alaska," he replied.

"We're far enough to the north that at certain times of the year, fall, in particular, we can see them, too."

They stared out the window in reverent silence for a long while, watching the roiling of the northern lights paint the sky. Eleanor felt him so near, his broad shoulder at her back, brushing against it. She closed her eyes and sniffed his scent—a combination of northern woods, leather, and tobacco, though she hadn't seen him smoking. She sniffed again and decided he didn't smoke cigarettes but likely tobacco in a pipe. Eleanor raised her eyes higher and met his intent gaze. Heat suffused her cheeks again when she realized she'd been watching him.

"Eleanor—"

"Riley," she said at the same time.

He took her in his arms and dipped his head, his gaze on her lips. Eleanor slowly lifted her arms up and around his waist, then higher, delighting in the muscles in his back. Lord, but it felt wonderful to feel him against her, and she tipped her head back, allowing his lips to settle on hers.

His kiss was gentle, tentative, a peck really, but enough that it ignited a flame in Eleanor she'd never experienced before. She tightened her arm around him and he deepened the kiss. After too short a time he released her and took a step back. She didn't like the fact he was frowning at the floor.

"Eleanor?" he said then, meeting her gaze. "I'm not sure this arrangement is going to work out between us."

She gasped, "Why not?"

"Because I want you—the way a man wants a woman—which is not the way a man should feel about his employer."

She bit her lip and crossed her arms across her breasts, unsure how to reply. Her heart beat rapidly in her chest. He liked her—apparently, he more than liked her! The feeling was mutual. But then sadness filled her. She had a feeling he wouldn't be able to stay and work for her if he had strong feelings for her in a romantic way, and she couldn't leave this place, not even for him. Still, she needed him to stay. If he didn't, she wasn't certain she could spend another lonely winter on her own, no matter how much she loved her home.

"Well, then, if you feel you must leave then there's not much I can do, is there?" she said, disappointment settling in.

"Who said anything about leaving?"

"Why, you said you don't feel about me as an employee should feel about his employer, didn't you?"

"Sure, I did, but I've a way to solve the problem."

Eleanor saw his lips form into a deep grin and she felt herself responding. "And what would that be?"

He took her into his arms again. "Seems the only thing I can do is marry you."

She laughed. "The only thing?"

"For now. Don't you agree?"

Eleanor nodded eagerly and laughed when he swept her up into his arms and twirled around in a circle. When he stopped he kissed her again and lowered her to the floor. He pulled her against him and held her for a long while.

Finally, he moved back, took her hand, and pulled her to the window again.

"Would you just look at that," he whispered.

"I am," Eleanor replied, her eyes focused only on him.

She would be safe, warm, and loved this winter. What more could she want? At this moment all of the sights in the northern sky weren't important to her—just Riley.

"It's something else, isn't it?" he asked.

"It most surely is," she replied, still looking at him, this man she would marry.

"Hey," he said, meeting her eyes. "You're not looking at the northern lights."

"No. I'm looking at something much, much better, husband-to-be."

"Ah, you're sure then."

"Yes, but are you?"

"From the minute I picked you up off the pavement I knew you were the lass for me."

Her eyes widened. "Truly?"

He nodded.

"When would you like to get married?"

"The sooner the better, don't you think?"

"Yes, absolutely, positively." She frowned then. "But are you certain you'll be able to live all year up here, being away from city life?"

He gathered her close, kissed her again, and murmured against her lips. "With you in my arms every night, yes. Where's the nearest preacher?"

"Down the road in Orting. Tomorrow soon enough for you?" she asked, pulling back from him to look into his eyes.

"Now. It has to be now."

"We won't find a preacher to marry us this time of night!"

She saw the sensual, glittery look in his eyes when he said, "You doubt my ability of persuasion?"

Shivers traveled up her spine as she looked at the set of his jaw, the dark, intent look of desire in his eyes. "No."

"Good." He stepped back from her, turned, and pushed her toward her bedroom door, aiming a playful slap to her bottom. "Then go put on your prettiest dress!"

❦

They arrived in Orting at midnight. Riley nearly broke down the preacher's door until the man answered. He took one look at Riley and promptly married them in his parlor, not in the church located right next door to his modest house. The poor preacher had to roost his tired wife from bed, but from the resigned look on her face, it likely wasn't the first time a couple wanted to marry in the middle of the night.

Eleanor made a beautiful bride, dressed in a sunny yellow day dress and a small straw hat perched on her head. The best clothing

Riley had was an old woolen rumpled suit jacket that had belonged to his father—dated, old—but perfect in Eleanor's eyes. He looked wonderful.

After the ceremony, they immediately drove home. When Riley opened the passenger door to let Eleanor out, he couldn't stop looking at her. He closed the door, picked her up in his arms, and she laughed as he carried her over the threshold.

Memories were made that night. But the memory that would remain foremost in Eleanor's mind, for all the days of her life, was the two of them, gazing up at the night sky in autumn as the myriad of lights from the aurora borealis entertained them, binding them together—forever.

THE END

Don't miss out on your next favorite book!

Join the Satin Romance mailing list
www.satinromance.com/mail.html

❦

THANK YOU FOR READING

❦

Did you enjoy this book?

We invite you to leave a review at your favorite book site, such as
Goodreads, Amazon, Barnes & Noble, etc.

DID YOU KNOW THAT LEAVING A REVIEW...

- Helps other readers find books they may enjoy.
- Gives you a chance to let your voice be heard.
- Gives authors recognition for their hard work.
- Doesn't have to be long. A sentence or two about why
  you liked the book will do.

ABOUT THE AUTHOR

NANCY PIRRI

Nancy Schumacher is the owner-publisher of Melange Books, LLC, writing under the pseudonyms, Nancy Pirri and Natasha Perry. She is a member of Romance Writers of America. She is also one of the founders of the RWA chapter, Northern Lights Writers (NLW), and is a member of Midwest Fiction Writers and Romancing the Lakes chapters in Minnesota.

www.nancypirri.com

Made in the USA
Las Vegas, NV
17 September 2022

55471025R00114